Heart Keeper

Heart Keeper

Keeper Trilogy
Book 2

Melanie Joye

Historical Romance by
Melanie Joye
from

Wisteria Publications

Wisteria Publications
507-4 Briar Hill Heights
New Tecumseth, ON
L9R 1Z7

Heart Keeper
ISBN: 978-1-988763-26-2
Copyright © 2021 by Melanie Joye

Published in Canada 2021

Layout and Cover Art by Taria van Weesenbeek
Back Cover Photo Credit: Melanie Climenhage

Please contact the author at jamn2@rogers.com for any questions or comments.

*Do not move an ancient boundary stone or encroach on the
fields of the fatherless*

Proverbs 23:10 - NIV

Keeper Trilogy

Secret Keeper Book One
Heart Keeper Book Two
Memory Keeper Book Three - Coming Soon

For Jim

Keeper Trilogy

MacEwen Keep

Fallon MacEwen

Lochlan MacEwen

Brianna MacEwen

Campbell Keep

Angus Campbell

Annella Campbell

Iain Campbell

Rose Keep

Justus De Ros

Caol De Ros

Bonnie of Rose

Davyd De Ros

Prologue

AD—1583, somewhere in the Scottish Highlands

When Justus De Ros returned to their bed chamber she was gone, no longer standing at her predictable place, by the west window, gazing into the predawn for . . . he knew not. Mayhap shadows, wisps of memories, ghosts of what had been but were no more.

She, standing there. Twas something he'd depended on since their exchange of marriage vows a fortnight ago. A single, lone figure, white night dress falling to her ankles, a dark braid—wisps of black hair pulled from it after a night's sleep—trailing down her back past her waist. Always a single thread, the predictability of it, pulled him to her. An enigma. And she was his.

De Ros closed his eyes for a moment, remembering the first time he had seen her stand there, at predawn, the morn after their marriage vows . . .

He went to her and stood with his shoulder resting against the window frame, looking at her.

"All is well," he reassured.

When she slid her eyes from the predawn grey and looked at him, the jolt that rattled his heart captured his breath. She veiled her sorrowful eyes quickly and when she looked back at him her silver eyes were the same misty greys of the fog that rose outside the window—unfathomable.

"Is all well, De Ros?" she replied and turned back to the window.

"Aye. Both bairns—Caol and Bonnie—sleep." He watched her for a time. A small woman, hands clasped in front of her, seemingly alone, remote, unfathomable—that word again. Then, he touched her, her braid just above the shoulder, and she had lifted those grey eyes and watched him as he slid his fingers along the silky plait until he held its end. Untying the leather strip that bound it, he unwound her hair, caressing the tresses, and spread them over her shoulders. His hands fell to his sides.

"Will you lie with me, Brianna?" Her name should be Breeze he had thought for he had detected a slight movement from her. Like a fluttering of a mild breeze that dances round you and then disappears. How long they stood there caught in the silence, he could not say.

"I am but a maid, De Ros." Her words came to him upon the lightening greys of the predawn, in the upswept lashes of her clear eyes, through the dispersing fog of the morn, on the trembling whisper of her breath.

"It will be new for both of us, together, Brianna." He touched her again, gently placing a hand atop her clasped ones, waiting.

Another flutter, a gentle breeze moved closer, caressing him. "Aye, De Ros." Her eyes fell to their hands and then followed their movement as he lifted them to his lips, kissing each.

At that moment, he had called on the angels themselves as he buried his anticipation for a bit longer. Only God knew how long he had waited for her—one year, two? Stamping down his desire to sweep her into his arms and carry her to the bed, he released her and walked to it, sitting on its edge, looking at her, waiting. Again waiting for her. Silently calling, yearning for her to come. Come close, breathe your breath upon me, dance with me, sweet Breeze. . .

A current of air wafting around his ankles brought De Ros from his musings. He squeezed his eyes shut several times for he had stared at that window, where his wife was not, for so long that his eyes had watered. A quick scan of the bed chamber told him again his wife was missing.

Where was his wife? He wanted her. These early morning hours always allowed for private time to talk, to be away from those two bairns—Caol and Bonnie—who crowded their bed at night and prevented him from touching his new wife in the way he wanted. This was their time now, to talk, to touch, to love. Where was Brianna? The cool air drifted around him again and he turned toward a soft creak. The door to the chamber tower was ajar.

De Ros ascended the stone steps two at a time, stepped through an arched entrance and onto the small tower platform. His stomach clenched. Brianna stood against the crenelated wall, her braid hanging down her back, her night dress fluttering about her feet, leaning outward peering through the notched space. He wondered if she was preparing to jump and moved closer. She stood very still, motionless, just gazing. The way she looked out the window each early morn in their chamber.

"Tis a chill in the air," he stated in his attempt

to move his wife from her motionless stance and away from the wall. He stood in his tunic that he had pulled on to carry the bairns from his bed and into their own chambers. But he knew there was no chill, for he could feel the summer heat from the ground rising and begin to penetrate through the mists that covered the valley below.

With his foot, De Ros snagged a small stool from the corner of the platform, dragged it an arm's length from his wife and then sat upon it. He pulled a small woven basket from the same corner and lifted out its contents—an old piece of wood and a small knife. He began to whittle the wood. Twas an activity that always calmed him and he felt himself relax. Again . . . he waited for her.

"Tis strange."

Her whispered words stilled his hands and he lifted his eyes to her.

"Tis a strange mixture—happiness and grief."

As she flicked a single finger on the stone wall, he saw a small print—a stain of blood. She had pressed her hand against the wall so hard that she had wounded her finger. He wanted to take her in his arms and kiss that finger, kiss . . . he could not. He waited.

"Tis strange to find such joy and wonder here, with you, in your arms . . . For certain, such happiness would not be mine if my brother, Fallon, had not been killed."

Stark and true words. Twas not how he had hoped to wed Brianna. Yet, days after Fallon had been murdered, she had been brought to his door step at Rose Castle for shelter and safety. They had married.

When she turned her head to him, the grief in her eyes jarred him to sit just a bit straighter on the stool.

"Tis a battle, De Ros, betwixt the two. Which do I lean into? Happiness or grief? Blessings or guilt? Each pulls me ever so hard."

Twas almost a relief when she turned away from him to peer again, endlessly, toward the west from where she had come. Where she had buried her brother.

De Ros continued to whittle and to think. Twas wise to say few words. Twas a mystery, this paradox. When he had lost his first wife and young daughter to the ague, he thought he would mourn forever. Twas strange how he had still found happiness in his young son, Caol, amidst the grief and pain. Twas what had pulled him from his own despair.

"When I was a young lad, I wanted to be a priest." His head snapped up at her boisterous laugh. He only knew her to be the serious young woman whom he had married a fortnight ago. Twas a new side to her. He peered a bit closer as she turned again toward him . . . his smiling bride?

"I do not think you could be a priest, De Ros. No, I think not." Brianna lifted her hand to her mouth to cover her smile and then turned again to the west. "The things you do in our bed, with me." She breathed deeply and exhaled and then her serious voice returned. "And why did you not become a priest?"

De Ros smiled at her back as she shook her head. "My father gave me a kick in my arse." He chuckled and then took on the voice of his father as he continued. "The eldest son is always raised to be the next Laird of Rose." He shrugged. "And now, I am the Laird of Rose."

He heard the laughter in her voice when she spoke again. "I wonder why you thought to be a priest."

"Twas the Scriptures, Brianna. The stories of the servant, Jesu." De Ros lifted the wood carving from his lap and continued to pare an end into a smooth point. "This God-man wanted to be a keeper of men's hearts. Twas an appealing notion to me. To guide men, to care for them, to keep their hearts safe."

"Tis a lovely idea, De Ros." Her laughter had faded and her whispered words floated gently away on the breeze.

Breeze. Twas who his wife was. A gentle wispy

breath of life whom he wanted to capture and hold. A wounded heart to bring back to life, to treasure, to keep. He breathed deeply to find the courage to ask his question, to declare his proclamation. "I thought about my predicament. A desire to be a priest and the demands of being a Laird. I realized that a Laird, too, is a guide for his people. One who cares for those in his realm."

Justus De Ros' heart beat too fast and his legs seemed weak as he rose and stepped beside her. He reached for his wife and turned her toward him and then opened his hand to reveal the tiny wooden sculpture he had carved. Her silver eyes fluttered to his face and then again to his hand to stare at the delicate wooden heart. "I want your heart, my Brianna, my Breeze." He raised his hand in offering. "My love, will you let me be the keeper of your heart?"

Chapter One

1600 AD—17 years later

Twas no large bird flapping along the high cliff eating grubs and seeds from the stone wall. Twas no piece of ripped cloth from a sail that had caught on a sharp edge of the stone cliff and billowed in the wind.

Indeed! As he watched carefully, the far-away greyish spot was slowly descending the cliff. "Hmm."

Caol had spied it as he had climbed over the rail of the small ship that had carried them north of the Scottish coast to the Islands of Orkney. His eyes had not left the movement on the cliff wall even as he settled into the skiff and sat motionless while his travel companion, Iain Campbell, rowed it toward shore. He was relieved that Campbell had not spied the woman descending the cliff wall. The man's back was to her as he gripped the oars, propelling the rowboat through the choppy waters. In all honesty, he would have no explanation for Campbell, or any person, as to why that woman scaled cliff walls.

As Caol continued to watch her descent, he felt his ire rising. He had taken her at her word, two years past, when she had promised him that she would end this dangerous activity.

The skiff hit a sandbar close to the shore and both he and Campbell jumped into the water and dragged the boat to higher ground. They had traveled to this location to purchase ponies. Twas not a task that Caol had desired, but his father had demanded it of him and now here he was on the shores of Vali Island. The ship that dropped them off would sail again through these waters in a fortnight and return them to mainland Scotland.

Caol turned to his companion. "I would walk along this shore alone for a time before I begin my visit here." Twas somewhat of a lame excuse. But Caol wished to rid himself of Campbell before he ventured to that cliff to catch that woman in her foolishness and wring her neck. He noticed Campbell's frown but the man remained silent as Caol continued. "At the low bush yonder is a path. Twill lead you to the foot trail that brings you atop the cliff. Once there, you will see a croft of stone and peat with a pointed roof. There live Alan and Ferna. Tell them I will be along shortly."

The frown did not leave Campbell's face as he lifted his pack and turned toward the path. Caol held his breath as the man walked past the low bush and turned right onto the trail.

Caol turned in the opposite direction, settled his pack on the ground and gazed narrow-eyed at the expanse of beach that led to her. Twas a good distance, indeed. Then he ran, sucking in great breaths of air as he hoisted himself over large boulders that sat along the shore. He sped across the sands and pebbles and propelled himself through a waterfall that poured from a spring high along the cliff edge. He stopped to catch his breath and pulled the leather cape dripping with water from his shoulders and laid it on the ground. He turned to the sea, measuring the level of the tide waters. Still quite low, yet the waters covered the land path. Irritated, he shook his head and then waded into the heaving waves, to waist deep, and journeyed around a jutting rock bend. The shore beckoned him once again and he waded onto its solid ground. He bent over, hands on his knees, breathing deeply and striving to contain his anger.

"Hmm. I am a fool," he muttered. "A besotted fool." He stood upright, anger churning in his gut, as he watched her final descent of about a hundred feet to the ground below. She had tucked her skirt into her waistband and something stirred within him as he gazed upon her shapely legs. He nudged the stray thought away as he strode toward her. "Fool," he growled.

When her toes touched the sand, he grabbed her at the waist and twirled her around so that she stood with her back pinned against the cliff.

"Imbec—" Her whispered word slid across her tongue and ended in a surprised squeak. "Caol!" she breathed, dragging her skirt hem from her waistband and positioning it rightly.

"Sheridan." His hands skimmed up her arms and rested gently on either side of her neck. Her beautiful neck that felt slightly damp from exertion. He felt his anger replaced by fear, coiling in his belly. Fear that always gripped him when he thought of her falling from these high cliffs and finding her wounded on the ground. He could barely allow that other word to venture into his thought. But there it was. *Dead.* His dear friend, *dead* on the ground.

Caol gave her a slight shake and strove to take the tremble from his voice. "You promised, Sheridan. You gave your pledge to me—no more climbing cliffs."

She raised her hands quickly and gripped his wrists. Twas his turn to be startled as Sheridan narrowed her eyes, their golden flecks flashing, and stared back at him. She puffed out a breath, readying to speak, he thought. But instead, she scrambled around him, appearing distraught. Or, was that fear shimmering low in her eyes? Confused, he turned to her. "Sheridan?"

She stood looking at him, hands clasped against her abdomen. She rubbed a thumb across the knuckles of the other. "Caol De Ros," she began quietly. "I would ask that you do not speak to me of promises. You were to arrive here, to Vali Island, in the early summer." She raised her face upward to the cliff edge, scanning its horizon. Fear glimmered in her eyes and trembled at her lips.

"The ponies, all of them, were slaughtered." She wiped a hand across her eyes. "Although some also died. A sickness. It spread through the herd late winter, early spring—twas very wet and cold. I begged Vali the Younger to provide me more time. I might have been able to save more." Again she wiped her eyes and then shook her head. "Only two young females remain." She raised her clasped hands to her chest, staring into his eyes. "If only you'd come when you promised, you might have been able to help us. Given us some of your mother's wisdom. What does Lady Brianna do when her ponies fall sick?"

Before he could reply, she turned her face away and pulled her cape tightly about her. "Let us not speak of promises, Caol De Ros."

Now was not the time to explain to Sheridan his reasons for arriving to this Island so late in the summer. He would have to find a more appropriate time to share with her the happenings at Rose Castle. The early spring had brought enemy attacks on his family's land. He had remained to aid in its protection.

Caol reached out and touched her elbow. "Sheridan, I—"

She spun toward him and took a single step. "Where were you? I waited so long." She scanned the top of the cliff again. "And could wait no longer. Tis the reason, I am scaling the cliff wall."

Her flashing eyes sobered as he quickly reached out to embrace her, holding her close, waiting for her taut body to loosen, for her fear—or was it anger?—to seep away. He vowed then that he would never challenge Sheridan on promises kept and promises broken.

"Caol?"

He smiled at the way his name skipped across her tongue. Twas melodic, a particular tone and cadence unique to her. "Aye, Sheridan."

"Vali the Younger. He is demanding that I wed him."

The jolt of anger that shot through Caol pushed Sheridan from him. He held her at arms-length, gripping her elbows to steady himself.

"He says I am to blame for the death of the ponies. That Alan and Ferna must pay recompense. Tis I, their daughter, that he wants. My talents and skills with the ponies. He says I can grow the herd back and help the Island to prosper again." She tapped her fingers against her temple, shaking her head. "His mind has become imbecile."

Caol widened his eyes at Sheridan's word. "Imbecile?" he muttered. Feeble-minded? Had it come to this? He supposed that Vali's ideas did, at times, teeter precariously toward foolhardiness.

"Tis why I was descending the cliff. Vali vows that when he returns to the Island on the morrow we will wed. He will not consider looking beyond this cliff. So, I will hide in a cave, over yonder." Sheridan took several steps along the shore and looked toward an unseen cave.

Caol pushed his fingers through his hair. His father had approached him several times to travel to Vali Island to purchase ponies. He had refused each time, only wanting to remain at Rose Castle and ensure its safety. The attacks this spring had commanded a heightened vigilance from all members of its community. He had led several searches to ensure that Rose Lands were free of danger. Even his foster sister, Bonnie of Rose, had fled to England to find safety with her new husband at his home— Braemoore. Much uncertainty still existed as to why Rose Keep had been attacked, but it appeared to be connected to his foster sister, Bonnie.

Twas strange that he now stood beside another young woman, much like his sister Bonnie, who also needed help, aid, rescue. A sense of relief seemed to ease the tension from his body as he realized that he was, in fact, pleased that he had, at last, accepted his father's request and journeyed to the Island. No ponies here. But Sheridan was here.

A few strides and Caol stood before her. His heart pounded too fast and his hands felt clammy. He would not have anticipated this moment in his final conversation with his father. Several of the ponies at Rose Castle had been sent to Braemoore as part of his foster sister's dowry. He had reassured his father that he'd bring back a stud pony to Rose Keep to grow their depleted herd. It appeared now that he would bring Sheridan back to Rose Keep instead.

"We will marry this day, Sheridan. Before Vali the Younger returns." He took her hand and turned her toward the path, toward her parents' home.

Sheridan tugged on his hand, stopping him, drawing him back to look at her. Her gaze intense, she held her lower lip between her teeth and stepped even closer to him. "Why, Caol? Why would you marry me?"

Her calm and quiet voice, melodious voice, danced around him, almost embracing him until . . . by God, what had he done? He took a step back and released her hand. His brow was damp and not because of his recent swim. Nay, twas damp from the surprise of her question. Or was it his question? He stared at her, speechless. How did he explain to Sheridan that he knew the number of freckles on her face, or that her eyes matched the colour of the dark streams and rivers of his home? Would he frighten her, scare her away, if he spoke of how he envisioned her lovely lips tilting into her shy smile when he lay awake at night, dreaming?

Caol's stomach tightened and his chest seemed to forbid him air. "I would offer you my protection, my name, Sheridan, if you would desire it. To help you through this strange predicament." Twas the only marriage proposal he had ever offered. To his ears, it sounded strange, lame he supposed, and rather cowardly. In these last few years he had not been able to find the courage to express his growing feelings for her.

Caol's heart pounded too hard as he studied Sheridan's narrow-eyed frown, her brows pulling together. She would refuse his offer? He stood taller, pulling his shoulders back, steadying himself for her rebuff, surprised at the nudge of pain close to his heart.

When he thought Sheridan might respond, she turned away and looked out to the sea. Her unbound hair—dark with blond tips painted by the summer sun—danced wildly about her as if keeping rhythm with the crashing waves upon the shore. He looked up to the cliff wall. Sheridan always wore a headband or kerchief to keep her curls in place. Mayhap she had lost it in her perilous descent down the side of the cliff. Disappointment poked at him. If she refused his proposal, he would never have a moment to run his hands through those tresses, the colours of the rich earth. Twas when Sheridan spun around and faced him, her lovely lips tilting into that shy smile, his heart soared with hope.

"So be it," Sheridan spoke, her whispered words swirling on the wings of the wind.

Caol nodded, wondering at his sense of relief now that she had accepted his proposal. "Come Sheridan, I would speak with your father, Alan." He and Sheridan must get on with it. They must marry before Vali's return. A swim around the rock bend, a walk through a water fall and a climb over some boulders would bring them to the trail that led to her home. As Caol took her hand and stepped toward that path, Sheridan stepped toward the rope that still hung from the cliff.

"Tis a shorter distance, Caol." She held onto the rope's end, her expression serious as she looked upward. "Expeditious."

Caol slid his eyes to his soon-to-be-wife,

pushing his hand through his hair. Sheridan's words! The woman loved trying out new words that she heard while trading produce at the dock. Did she know that it always captured his attention the ways those words skipped off her tongue so smoothly, the lilt of her voice frolicking about him? It waylaid him, made him lose his thought, made him want to kiss her lips, tasting her mouth, caressing . . .

"Hmm." He peered closer. Sheridan looked upward and pulled on the rope, appearing oblivious to the spell she and her words cast over him. Expeditious rot! Never would he climb up or down that rock wall! Indeed the first opportunity he got, he would sever that rope.

"Nay, Sheridan," he countered. "We will take the path to your parents' croft." He pulled her along by her hand to the water's edge. "A short swim around this bend and then a walk along the shore. Tis the safe way."

Sheridan looked back at the rope, then pulled her skirt between her legs and tucked it into her waistband. Jumping over a wave, she waded into the water and laughed as the next wave toppled her over.

Caol chuckled as Sheridan dove into the water, her skirted bottom the final part to disappear beneath the water. Something stirred deep within him. His smile widened. She would be his this eve.

"Besotted fool," he muttered.

Chapter Two

Sheridan smiled at the merry-makers as she walked beside Caol along the path toward her marriage croft. Oh, how she loved these dear people. The marriage and dinner had been a fine celebration. Now, as they neared the end of the festivities, some Islanders beat sticks, a few pounded on drums. The light from the small lantern she held and the torches carried by a few men swayed rhythmically. A young boy played a lovely stream of notes on a flute while children danced around her and Caol. Many sang and, now and again, a few lewd remarks rose above the clamour. Even through all this noise, she was sure she heard Angel singing too. The strains of her flute adding levity to this eve.

A quiver radiated from her heart when Caol took her hand and brushed his thumb across her palm. Sheridan was glad the twilight hid the blush that heated her face. Twas the first time Caol had ever touched her in an intimate way. Only friends they had been, until a few hours past when they had exchanged vows. Now they were husband and wife.

Twas hard to believe that she was Caol's wife. To be sure, the thought made her dizzy. Never in her imagination would she have anticipated his offer of marriage. But she had known, as she stood on the beach trying to find the courage to accept his proposal, that the only solution to her predicament was Caol. She had known this all through the summer as she had yearned for Caol to come—*come Caol to Vali Island*—her heart had sung. Her hope, her faith in his imminent arrival, had slowly faded as each summer day had passed by, as the daylight slowly ebbed and twilight grew longer.

Vali the Younger had pestered her throughout these days. To be sure, he had even tried to court her and brought her flowers once. Never could she marry the man who had murdered the ponies! Melancholia caressed her heart. Dear ponies. Finally Vali had declared they would wed. She shivered at the thought. She would explain the entire predicament to Caol on the morrow.

But for now, she delighted in the giddiness of being Caol's wife. Her feelings for him ran deep, rooted within years of wandering the Island together each summer when he had visited with his father. The caresses slowly lessened as Caol tightened his grip on her hand. She peered down the pathway to their marriage croft, sensing her husband's suspicion. Casually Caol lifted a hand and grasped the handle of his sword that rested at his back. To be sure, twould be a perfect place for Vali's men to accost them. Sheridan nibbled on her lower lip, scanning the shadows as she walked beside her husband.

Even though they had striven to keep their wedding ceremony quiet, even secret, once the priest was called to bless their union, people from Sheridan's village began to arrive at her parent's cottage. Twas only a matter of time word would travel to Vali's family. Would his men try to stop this marriage consummation now or would she face Vali's temper on the morrow? Sheridan breathed deeply, struggling to find her calm—that quiet place of tranquility that barred entrance to confusion.

Sheridan's heart skipped a beat when they stopped in front of the door of the small croft. All appeared very calm, even the ferns seemed to be sleeping. She smiled at the little abode that had been her dear grandmother's.

"You will receive this croft when you marry, Sheridan," her Mormor had always told her. And so it was. Twould be a lovely place to celebrate her wedding night. So many fond memories lingered here.

"Caol!" she screeched as her new husband swung her into his arms. She laughed as the merry-makers roared encouragement to Caol, clapping and bellowing into the night. Caol pushed open the door of the small croft with his foot and carried Sheridan over its threshold. He turned around and stood full in the doorway, grinning broadly at the merry-makers who shoved and pushed to enter the small croft too. Then he bowed his head and snagged the door with his foot, closing it on their startled faces.

Sheridan stared at Caol, shocked. Twas not proper to close the door on her people. "Tis tradition, Caol, to allow them in to light the fire at the hearth and to bless the marriage bed." She struggled in his arms to escape and at least bid the merry-makers a polite good eve.

"Nay, Sheridan." Caol lowered her down to stand beside him. "Tis a strange ritual that you Islanders have." He reached around her to the door and pulled the latch into its wooden lock. Her back was pinned against the door and Caol leaned into her, arms extended on either side of her head, a twinkle of humour in his eyes. "We Scots require no help in making our own fire." When he smiled, she was sure the heat on her face rose to her hairline.

Caol placed the small lantern that she clutched in her hand on a wooden stand and walked to each of the shuttered windows, checking the latches. Twould be just like Vali to attempt to enter the croft through a door or window. Caol turned again to her, took a couple of strides and pulled her toward the small cot that sat next to the hearth. "By dawn's light, we will have blessed our marriage bed," he crooned.

Sheridan exhaled a soft, nervous laugh, as she walked into her husband's embrace. A skitter of anticipation radiated across her breast and joy leapt within her heart. She had thought she would spend this night hidden in the cave absolutely unsure of what the morrow would bring. Earlier, relief had washed over her when she had touched the ground at the bottom of the cliff and spun around, only to look into Caol's eyes. Sheer joy. The same joy that danced around her now as her lips parted beneath his. Sheer wonder cradled her as she wrapped her arms around Caol's neck, snuggling closer in his arms.

Sheridan followed Caol's hands with her own, resting them lightly at his wrists as he began to undo her belt that sat across her torso from shoulder to waist. It held the sword that hung at her back.

"You will not be needing this sword this eve," Caol whispered against her ear as he untied the tightly woven belt that was intricately designed with various colours of wool. "Nor this one," as he guided her hands to his leather belt.

They each held the other's sheathed sword. Caol pulled hers from its scabbard, knelt and laid it on the dry dirt floor between them. When he raised his head and looked at her, waiting, she stared in amazement. He would honour her by participating in this tradition of her Island. She laughed softly again as she hoisted his sword from its sheath and lowered it to the ground. Warmth filled her as Caol guided her hands.

Crossed swords. The sacredness of their union.

"I pledge my oath that I will stand with you, fight for you and protect you, Sheridan, until our days are no more," Caol whispered.

Before she could untangle her thoughts and respond, his lips opened over hers and he absorbed the words of her unspoken pledge. She melted into the fragrance and taste of Caol, a sea breeze of salt and the wildness of the ocean winds. Then she rose with him as he pulled her toward the hearth. He knelt before her to remove her boots and set them before the hearth, a symbol of their new home. He was honouring another of her Island traditions. Twas why she loved Caol. He had always shown a thoughtfulness toward her, as if he could sometimes know what she was thinking. He knew she held her Island traditions dear.

Oh, how happy she now was that her new husband had refused the merry-makers entry, for her fire was warming. Its glow rose higher as Caol's hands caressed along her ankle and upward to her knee. He loosened the first boot and slid it from her foot. He pulled a small dagger from the inside pocket of the boot and tossed it toward the crossed swords.

"You will not be needing that this eve," he stated, looking at her with such intensity that her hand reached out and gripped the mantel for balance.

When Caol's hands caressed under her skirts again, the fire smouldering in her belly leapt. He tugged the second boot from her foot.

"Neither will you be needing this dagger." When his eyes slid to her, Sheridan was sure she would melt into him, into his dark eyes that called to her like the caves along the cliffs, beckoning her to come closer and explore.

She clutched the mantel tighter as his hands rose higher under her skirt, on her bare legs. Exploring above her knees, higher and higher, caressing her thighs. His thumbs swirling, the heat pooling, their fire blazing hot.

Her eyes snapped open, for his hands had ceased their climb. She swallowed hard to tamp her fire as Caol untied her garter secured high on her right thigh. Twas where she carried a third and final dagger. The rattling of the tossed knife echoed as Caol gripped the back of her knees, pulling her down onto his lap where she straddled him.

Her heart skipped a beat as he smiled at her and looked down at their position, for her skirt sat bunched at her waist and he had pulled his tunic aside.

"I will be the only sword . . ." he whispered as he pulled her closer to him "and you, the only sheath, as we create our own traditions and rituals this eve." Oh, how the flames rose around her as Caol nestled his lips against her neck, placing velvety caresses downward and reached for the laces at her bodice.

The fire licked Sheridan's fingertips as she ran her hands beneath his tunic lifting it over his head. The heat scorched her hands as she lay them against his muscled chest and down along his arms to his hands. She rested them gently at his wrists as he loosed her gown and then pulled the ribband that secured the chemise at her neck.

As her clothes fell from her shoulders, and her blouse and skirt swept away, Caol touched her breast so gently, a single caress, that Sheridan's pulse leapt like a hot spark into the night. She pulled Caol down with her onto the sheep skin rug that lay before the dark hearth.

She breathed deeply in anticipation, as his hands stroked along either side of her body. Then he framed her face with them, touching her tenderly, softly.

Caol's breath of sea and salt whispered across her face. "Twill be my tradition, my ritual, to be forever the keeper of your heart, Sheridan." And then his mouth and his hands were on her, on her mouth, on her face, along her neck.

Their fire soared, it crackled, exploded and she flew with Caol and the million sparks high into the heavens.

Chapter Three

His eyes opened at the crack of thunder.

Confused, Caol stared at the ceiling above, remembered, and then smiled at all that had occurred in this croft last eve. Now twas damp and cold within this small abode of sod and stone, unlike last night when he and Sheridan had built their own heat, their own fire. In fact, that fire still smouldered and he turned toward his new bride to stir their fire. Gone! Her sword still lay on the dirt floor crossed with his, yet all her knives . . . vanished along with his wife.

The thunder shook the small hut again, pounding at the door and pummeling the shuttered windows. It seemed the raging storm circled directly above this croft. As he rose from the cot, a great racket of thunder flung him back onto the bed. Twas as though the storm was coming through the door and the windows. Indeed, twas true. The door banged open and the shutters broke away from their leather hinges.

"Bloody Hell!" Caol bellowed above the clatter as Vali the Younger strode in through the open croft door. Two of Vali's men climbed in through the windows. Sunlight followed the intruders into the room. Caol rose and took a single step toward his sword only to halt when Vali's men pulled their swords from their scabbards and stepped toward him.

"Bloody hell, Vali. Have you lost all sense, man?" But possibly it was he, Caol De Ros, that had lost all sense. Indeed, so lost in the memories of last night he had been unable to distinguish between a thunder storm and a group of maniacs pounding at his door. Caol sneered at the sunlight and then rubbed his hands over his face. Twas only when his tunic was tossed to him, landing on his head that he came fully to his senses.

"Damn it, Vali," he snarled, realizing he stood in the middle of the small croft stark naked. "Did you give no consideration that my wife might be here with me?" He pulled his shirt over his head, pushing his arms through the sleeves.

"Tis why we pounded for as long as we did, Caol. To give the Island's new married couple time to prepare for our entry." Vali looked around the small room. "Appears your wife is already out and about." He nodded toward the two guards and they exited the croft through the door.

Caol clenched his hands, glaring at the man who stood just inside the door. Vali must have spent the night drinking on the ships for the aroma of alcohol wafted from him and dark shadows sat below his blood-shot eyes. As Caol looked to his sword to retrieve it, Vali's dagger pierced the dirt floor before the hearth. Caol slid his gaze to Vali.

"You are playing a fool this day, Vali the Younger," began Caol, slow and deliberate in an attempt to tamp down his growing ire. "Speak your piece."

Vali's expression darkened. "Surely Sheridan has explained the challenges on the Island."

"Aye. You slaughtered the ponies and attempted to force Sheridan into marriage with you."

Vali's mouth dropped open and he took a single step back as if Caol's accusation might topple him. "Caol." Vali took a deep breath and straightened his back. "Vali the Elder died in late winter."

Now it was Caol's turn to step back and sit on the cot. Twas unbelievable. When he and his father, Justus de Ros, left the Island last summer, Vali the Elder appeared well and hardy.

"My father was laid to rest at the northern point of the Island. There he can watch the ships come and go and choose the one that will take him into the afterlife." A tinge of sadness mingled with Vali's bitter words.

Caol speared his fingers through his hair and allowed his grief for Vali the Elder to pierce his heart. Why had Sheridan not shared this part of the story? Twas an important occurrence when the Lord of an Island passed.

Caol stood and stared at Vali for a time. Vali and his brother, Petter, had been his boyhood friends with whom he had wandered the Island each summer for many years. "Take me to his final resting place."

Caol snagged his plaid and wrapped it around himself. He lifted his sword off the dirt floor, shoved it into its scabbard and strapped it on. Pulling on his boots, he noted the dagger nestled within each boot pocket. Thank God. Something brewed beneath Vali's hardened exterior, more than grief and anger. Something deep and fervent and intensely dark. Caol prayed that he would not have to use his weapons against his friend. For certain, whatever was amiss on this Island could be resolved with him and Vali working together. He snatched his cape from the cot and when he turned again to Vali, the door was still ajar and the croft empty.

As Caol strode through the hut doorway, sunlight, warm and bright, blasted his senses bringing him more fully into the happenings of this day. Iain Campbell stood a short distance from the croft.

Strangely, his pack was on his back and the guards held his sheathed sword. A snarl on Iain Campbell's face and a bruise over his left eye and another beside his mouth were tell-tale signs that he had not relinquished his sword willingly. "Hmm." A man's weapons were as essential as the air he breathed. Iain had accompanied him to the Island to purchase a pony or two. How did that deserve a beating? What, on earth, was going on here, on this godforsaken Island?

"This way," Vali commanded from atop a small knoll beside the croft.

Caol's hands tingled as he stared at Vali. Deep within him, he had such an urge to throttle the new Lord of this Island. Vali's demands of Sheridan, his unwelcome entry into their marriage croft and now the bruises on Iain Campbell's face called for retribution.

"Must I have your weapons too, Caol de Ros?" Two more guards appeared by Vali's side. "Or will you follow willingly?"

Caol eyed Iain Campbell a final time. As guards pushed Iain forward, Caol strode toward Vali and toward the final resting spot of Vali the Elder.

Two guards led the way to the north point of the Island. Caol fell into step beside Vali. Behind him, Iain Campbell followed reluctantly and two guards took up the end of the line.

"We were expecting your arrival in early

summer, Caol," Vali said. "You are late."

"Hmm," Caol growled. Rose Keep had been so focused on protecting its lands and its people this spring, there had been little time to send a missive north to alert Vali Island. "It would be usual to receive tidings from this Island to tell us of Vali the Elder's death," Caol countered. "How is it that we received not one missive?"

"Ah. Then let us begin this story at its start, shall we Caol?" Vali's voice simmered with anger. He stared straight ahead as he strode along the path toward Vali the Elder's grave. "Upon my father's death, strangely, two things occurred. A mare became ill and died. We believed this was the only sick animal. Yet within a fortnight, the disease spread throughout the herd. Twas a gruesome illness to watch. We strove to save some. And yet, most had to be slaughtered. Only two mares live." Vali sneered and shook his head. "Some Island folk believe the ponies mourned my father's death, choosing to follow him into the afterlife." He snorted, a thin critical sound. "Some of our people believe the Angel of the Island whisked the ponies away. All for rot, these fanciful superstitions."

As long as Caol could remember, superstitions abounded about the Angel of the Island. Some had sworn they had seen it. Twas an Island myth sometimes used to scare the children into obedience.

"If you don't listen, the Angel will whisk you away!" Even Vali the Younger had attempted to scare him when they were young lads. "Make sure you cover your head with blankets in your bed or the Angel of the Island will find you and carry you away." For a time, the boy Caol had believed the scary notion. Now, Caol recognized the myth as a fanciful fairy tale about a ghostly figure dressed in white, shimmering in the moonlight, who walked amongst the ponies.

Caol looked sideways at Vali and chose to remain silent. His question about a missive seemed to heighten Vali's ire and if he wished to keep his weapons he would say little more to provoke Vali. While he knew he could defend himself and his weapons against one or two men, Caol reckoned he could not against five—Vali and his four guards. Campbell had been rendered useless without his sword. Although . . . he looked behind at Campbell and then downward to his boots. All men carried hidden knives.

"We took every weapon we could find from Campbell."

Twas not just for a sword that Campbell had received his bruised face. When Caol turned to the new Lord of Vali Island, his clenched fists burned to punch him.

"Campbell is a fighter," Vali said with a

malicious grin. "He would not give over his weapons willingly."

There was a challenge in Vali's eyes and in his voice. He was not the man Caol had bade farewell to last summer and all the past summers when he and his father had visited. Indeed, Vali the Younger was a sullen man. Yet, now a cruel and hardened man walked beside him.

"The second incident that occurred after my father's death involved my role on this Island," Vali continued. "A small group of rebellious Islanders rose up and challenged my leadership. They were spreading corrupt ideas that I slaughtered the ponies without cause and ruined their livelihood. That I am no leader."

An hour's walk had brought them to the top of the pathway where they stood before a vast rock plateau. Caol could see the Elder's cairn in the distance. Vali strode towards his father's grave and Caol followed. A noise behind him caused him to look back. Iain Campbell was barred from following them and now stood sullenly with two guards on either side. Vali appeared not to notice.

"They are a bothersome group of men, small in number, possibly five," Vali continued. "You would recognize some from our boyhood days. Most work on the ships and they are disturbing the people with rumours and insidious lies. A few of them sit on the

Island Elder Council and are insisting on a vote to determine my leadership status. Tis possible that the Lordship of this Island may change hands."

Caol studied Vali for a time. Twas no good for any clan to have an angry, cruel leader. Caol had witnessed such leadership over the years amongst some of the mainland clans. Brutal leadership always led to failure. Possibly replacing Vali with another, more capable individual would be the way for this Island to venture forth.

"A missive was sent to Rose Lands, Caol." Anger sparked amongst Vali's words. "We had anticipated your arrival weeks ago, certain that your mother, Lady Brianna, would journey to our Island to assist with the illness infesting the herd." Vali shook his head and turned to the cairn that stood a few feet from them. "My father was always sure that your people would venture forth to help us if necessary. Twas a false assumption." He stepped close to the cairn and brushed his hands across several stones, sweeping debris off the sacred memorial.

Caol touched his hand to his head and chest and then to each shoulder, performing this solemn act for Vali the Elder. Twas strange the Elder had been buried rather than burned and set adrift to sea as was the tradition of this Island. He hoped the man had found his way successfully to the afterlife.

"Rose Keep did not receive your missive, Vali. Indeed, if it had, even then we would not have been able to send help." Caol wondered if the missive had been intercepted by the gang of men who threatened Rose Castle this early spring.

The warm sun shone upon this barren piece of rock, radiating its heat. Caol envied the long drink of water Vali took from his leather flask. "Rose Lands were infiltrated this spring by a gang of assailants. Strange happenings occurred, all connected to my sister, Bonnie. All men of Rose Keep were needed to defend the land and to ensure my sister's safe journey away from Rose Lands." Caol wiped the sweat from his brow. "My father would not have allowed my mother, Lady Brianna, to venture north to help your Island. I am sorry but our clan was directed to stay within Rose Lands for protection until the danger could be resolved."

Vali took another swig of water and wiped his mouth with the back of his hand. When he looked again at Caol, the bitterness that had etched his face had lessened. "I assumed Rose Keep had received my missive and had chosen not be involved with the problems on our Island." Vali shook his head and then shrugged. "When you did not appear in early summer, which is your usual custom, I thought . . . I withdraw my accusations, Caol. I should have recognized that something was amiss. And your sister, Bonnie. Did she find safety?"

"Aye. Her life was threatened. Unknown assailants wished her dead. But now all is well with my foster sister." Caol thought it best not to reveal to where Bonnie had fled. Bonnie's secrets had been protected at Rose Keep for seventeen years.

"Foster?" Vali questioned. "I have not met Bonnie but I always thought she was your sister by blood." He wiped his brow and again lifted the water flask to his mouth.

"Aye," Caol said. "She was a foundling wrapped in a seal-skin, discovered at the door of an old woman's cottage about twenty years past and brought to Rose Keep to —"

"Twenty years past!" Water spewed from Vali's mouth and flew onto Caol. Vali pounded at his chest, attempting to catch his breath, coughing and wheezing, choking on the water.

Caol smacked the man on his back, making Vali stumble forward several steps and lean down over his knees, breathing deeply. He had struck Vali harder than was necessary, yet the clout was instinctively given as retribution for Sheridan's fear and Iain's bruises and even Caol's growing temper which was made worse by lack of water. In the olden days, the friends always offered water and food to the other when they were exploring the Island. Vali's refusal to share water was another sign of his changed and bitter temperament.

Vali pulled himself up and turned to Caol, squinting. "Tis a risky business to pummel the Lord of the Island."

Caol grabbed Vali's shirt front so that they stood nose to nose. "Tis a risky business to threaten Sheridan with marriage, instilling her with fear!" He pushed Vali away. "I must find my wife. We will prepare and leave the Island. There is no more for us here. I know not if Rose Keep will continue to do business with you. But, send a missive when your herd has been grown again." As Caol walked away, a dagger flew past his right ear and landed at his feet.

"Nay," Vali yelled at Caol's back. "You will be staying on this Island until the two mares are returned."

Caol turned slowly toward Vali, confusion replacing his anger. Mares missing? He felt as though they had walked a full circle and were at the beginning of this strange conversation. "I will say it again Vali, say your piece."

"Your wife stole away the two surviving mares in the herd. She believed they would be slaughtered and gave me not a chance to observe them to determine their fate." Vali's words simmered again with anger. "They are hidden on the Island. I believed I knew every inch of this rock but cannot determine where she has taken them. I would have them returned. If they are healthy we can again grow our herd and thrive from this livelihood."

"Sheridan has spoken of the ponies but I knew not that she had taken them," Caol replied.

Vali's malicious smile appeared again. "Guards watch this Island carefully, Caol. I am told that you came onto the Island yesterday, late afternoon. By early evening you and Sheridan were married. I think that likely you and your bride had more on your mind than two hidden ponies."

Caol rubbed a hand through his hair. Vali's words were true. From the moment he had stepped foot onto this Island, circumstances had taken hold of him and, with little discussion, had pushed him into a marriage. "I do not understand why you would demand Sheridan to marry you, Vali."

"Where have you been, man? Have you not been listening to me?" Vali bellowed. "The challenges of the Island have been ongoing since early spring. The rebels want the ponies too. They are attempting to find their location and to take this livelihood as their own and away from the people. It is their stronghold toward power and wresting the Lordship from me. Sheridan has refused to reveal their location, either to me or to them. If they accost her, I suspect she will be forced to reveal the ponies' location and if she refuses, be greatly harmed. Sheridan chooses not to trust me, her life-long friend. Yet she is not safe. I am the Lord of this Island. I would marry her simply to give her protection whether she wants it or not. Caol, these rebels are nasty, unruly men."

Caol looked out to the sea. Twas a clear, bright day. If only Vali's story offered as much clarity. The man had always been full of guile. To be certain, from their boyhood days, a liar. Something was amiss. Sheridan had explained that Vali would force her to marry him to grow back the herd, that he blamed her for their deaths. Yet Vali explained that he offered to wed Sheridan to protect her? "Hmm," he muttered. And why on earth would the rebels believe the power to Lordship came through the ponies? Twas odd. The ponies brought meagre earnings to this poor and almost forgotten Island.

Caol placed his hands on his belt and turned his gaze to Vali. "Now, I stand in place for my wife. You will stay away from her and deal only with me. I will speak to Sheridan about these problems."

Vali took a step closer. "You will know, by my authority, your wife will not leave the Island until the ponies' location is revealed. Now that you have chosen to be Sheridan's husband, neither will you be allowed to leave the Island. The issue of the ponies must be resolved." Vali looked back to Iain Campbell. "Your companion will not be allowed to remain. I want no strangers on the Island until all has been settled." When Caol frowned, ready to protest on Campbell's behalf, Vali took a step closer to him. "Nay, I do not know this man who calls himself Iain Campbell or if he can be trusted. He will be given voyage to return to the mainland."

Begrudgingly, Caol admired Vali's authoritative approach to the Island's problems. Even he, who was the son of the Laird of Rose Keep, was regularly called upon to make decisions and extend authority over the lands and peoples. He would agree to Vali's decisions and help resolve this situation but only for Sheridan's sake.

Caol turned toward Iain Campbell who was already being led away by the Island guards.

"Caol!" Vali commanded.

"I would bid Campbell godspeed on his travels," Caol stated over his shoulder as he strode away. Vali gave a high pitched whistle and Caol saw the guards turn toward their leader. Vali must have signaled with a hand and they allowed Campbell to walk toward Caol unescorted.

In that moment, when Caol knew all eyes were on Vali, he ripped the leather strip tied at his neck and held it hidden in his hand.

"I knew naught of the problems on the Island until this morning," Caol said when he reached Iain. He thought that Campbell's expression softened a bit. "With the happenings at Rose Keep this spring, we knew not that there was trouble here, also." Caol extended an arm in salutation to Iain Campbell in hopes that the gesture would show his sincerity. "I give you my word. I speak truth."

Campbell studied Caol for a moment, then grasped his friend's arm. "I accept your word and will leave the Island peacefully."

Campbell's response gave Caol reassurance that his plan might work. The guards were approaching and were just a few yards from them. Caol must act quickly. As he withdrew his arm from Campbell, he patted him on the chest and tucked the leather strip into the fold of Iain's plaid. Now the guards stood on either side of Campbell.

"Godspeed on your travels, Iain Campbell," Caol stated.

Campbell frowned for a moment, then nodded at Caol and turned away to follow the guards toward the path that led to the sea.

Chapter Four

Sheridan lay on her stomach in a grassy field across from the plateau where Caol and Vali stood. She loved coming here, to Vali the Elder's final resting place. Yet today, as she was returning to the small croft she now shared with Caol, she had heard the commotion outside its door. She had slipped away and hid. Cowardly, she supposed.

Exasperated, Sheridan laid her head on her hands. The grass swaying in the wind tickled her nose. Over these past many weeks, she was spending more and more time in hiding. To be sure, too much hiding. She had too much to protect and too much to lose.

She blew out her breath in one long puff. She was tired. She would have escaped the Island if it had been possible. But she could not leave the ponies. And never could she leave her Angel. She had hidden the ponies with her Angel. So safely tucked away no one would find them unless she allowed it.

Sheridan had thought her plan wise, even when her parents had tried to convince her otherwise. Without realizing it, her plan had thrust her into hiding, too. First from Vali and then from the rebellious group of men who were challenging Vali's authority.

For reasons that she could not fathom, the ponies had become the focal point for the rebels' cause. "Vali has not handled the sickness well," they said. "The Island had lost some of its livelihood." Their words made little sense to her. Each year, the mares were bred. Yet the herd remained small and profit gained from selling the foals was a pittance. Twould seem that the rebels could find no other cause to gripe about. The other industries with which the Island sustained itself—sheep and wool, fishing and farming and the crafts created and bartered—were successfully existing. The ponies should be of little concern to the rebels. Why were the ponies of such interest to them? Until the chatter about them calmed, the ponies would remain hidden.

Sheridan raised her head, keeping her eyes just above the grass line to watch the men. She slapped a hand over her mouth as Caol hit Vali on the back and the men began to fight. It broke her heart to see the two friends at odds.

Guilt nudged Sheridan and she shook her head.

She had not really explained to Caol the whole story of these past many weeks. Bits and pieces, is all she had provided.

How was it that when she was around Caol, her thoughts got all in a muddle? With him, she just could not always find the words to express her ideas and thoughts. And the problem of the hidden ponies was only half of the story. Twas also the secret of her Angel that she knew she had to share with Caol. Twas hard to share a secret that had been hidden away for twenty years.

Yesterday, when Caol had caught her climbing down the cliff, her frustration drove the words to just spill out. Even she was surprised at her outburst. Before she knew it, she had married Caol. Throughout the wedding celebrations and into the early hours of the evening, there had been no time or opportunity to explain everything to Caol.

And then last night, their wedding night, all sane thoughts had flittered away. Sheridan rolled over on her back and gazed up at the early morning sky. She felt as dreamy, as light and lofty, as the white puffy clouds that slowly drifted overhead. Since her childhood, she had dreamed of only Caol. Over the years, they had bonded in friendship. Perhaps her silence and his boisterousness balanced each other.

Sheridan held her hand to her heart. Oh, how

it had soared when Caol had said, "We will marry this day." She had turned to the sea to hide her joy in the wild wind and the rhythmic roar of the waves pounding in jubilation. She could hardly believe her good fortune. Caol De Ros had actually offered her marriage.

For her, last night had been the culmination of the many years she had dreamed of being with Caol, as his wife. They had set some of their own traditions last eve. She giggled. To be sure, they had finally blessed the marriage bed.

The sound of a whistle pierced the air and Sheridan quickly rolled onto her stomach to peek above the tall grass. Twas Vali's habit, to communicate and command. She watched carefully as Caol strode away from Vali and toward the man, Campbell. When Vali raised his hand, signaling to his guards, Campbell approached Caol. A short conversation between them and then Campbell was led away.

For a time, Sheridan watched her husband. He did not move from his spot even when Vali and the guards disappeared down the trail. It was as if he looked beyond the cliff to the waves splashing against the shore for answers to the troubles Vali had told him about. Yet to reveal the location of the ponies, she would have to tell Caol about her Angel. That was the real trouble.

But twas time. Time! She drew in a deep breath, determined to tell Caol the whole story. But as Caol slowly turned in a full circle, her courage skittered away and she ducked lower in the grass, watching.

Caol stood tall, hands resting at his belt, legs apart, appearing to stare straight at her. Surely he could not guess that she was here, hiding so close. Once Caol had left, she would hurry to their croft and speak with him there.

Sheridan waited, watching for Caol's departure. The wind ruffled his dark hair, and pressed his tunic and plaid against the outline of his body. Sheridan trembled and captured her lower lip in her teeth. Twas hard to believe that she had held this formidable man in her arms last night, loving him. She wondered if she might ever share her true feelings with him.

She shook her head, attempting to focus on this precarious situation. She had some explaining to do and had to unmuddle her thoughts.

"Tis no tall piece of grass blowing in the wind," Caol declared loudly. "Tis your kerchief flapping above your head."

When she raised her hand to catch the end of the fluttering scarf, she knew she had been found and rose to sit cross-legged in the grass. "Caol," she whispered, heart beating ever so loud.

"Sheridan." He walked briskly toward her.

She pulled herself up from the grass and stood, measuring the pace of the hunter, who approached his prey, sober and calculating. A warm flush spread across her breast and her stomach fluttered in anticipation.

Twas the disappointment etched across Caol's face that made her throat seize and she coughed. In all truth, the secret she had tucked inside herself for all these years was difficult to pull out and share with this man and his intimidating stance. She scanned the area. A walk to a quiet spot would be a perfect way for her to ponder, to find the words to share with Caol.

"Come, Caol. We will walk."

She did not wait to hear Caol's muttered response. Rather, she turned away and jogged along a winding path toward the west. His heavy steps behind her echoed her own weighty thoughts. She skipped off the trail and walked a short distance to a deep water hole. There, she sat alongside its edge, her back against a large boulder and pulled her legs tightly to her chest, awaiting Caol to join her. Twas a perfect place for her to tell the whole story.

Whump.

Sheridan turned her head sharply. One of Caol's boots lay on the ground beside her. When she looked up to the edge of the boulder, a second boot was spinning downward, followed by his plaid. Next his tunic floated over the brink and landed gently on her shoulders. And finally Caol, naked Caol, plunged downward, arms and head first, diving into the water.

The man loved the water. Fearless in it, was he, like a boat plunging into its depths. His arms and head the bow, his feet the stern. She giggled. The mast of Caol's ship, fully on display.

His head popped up above the churning surface of the water. Twas a small pool but deep, a favourite swimming hole when they had been children.

"Tis been a trying morning," Caol began. "I awoke to a thunderstorm."

She narrowed her eyes and puckered her lips. "Thunderstorm? The mists lifted early, Caol, allowing the sun to shine." She pulled his tunic from her shoulders and hugged it to her breast. "Twas a dream then?"

"Twas a thunderstorm, Sheridan, rattled our croft. It would have been fine to have held on to you through it." He swam closer, then stilled. "But I found myself all alone." Disappointment still lingered about his eyes.

"I went for my morning ablutions," she explained. "When I returned, I saw the confusion at the croft." She could not bring herself to admit aloud, but her fear had kept her from sight.

Caol swam closer so that his feet touched the

bottom. The water level fell to his chest. "I can understand why you would not trust Vali to tell him where the ponies are. A vile temper has overtaken him." He took a step closer and the water level fell to his waist. "It would have been fine to hear the story from your lips."

She twisted the tunic in her hands, wringing it into a coiled rope. "Much has happened in this last day." She was shaking her head as if that would release the words she so wanted to say. With a shrug of her shoulders, she fell silent, staring at her hands.

"Hmm."

Sheridan raised her head to stare at Caol. That sound always indicated Caol didn't quite agree.

He raised his eyebrows ever so slightly, stepping a bit closer. The water level lowered to his hips. He reached out a hand to her. "Come. Swim with me." And then he smiled.

Away flittered her fear and confusion. How did her husband do that with just a simple smile? She smiled too, jumping up. It had been years since she had swum with him.

Sheridan moved quickly to the water's edge, lifted her skirt to tug her boots off and then tossed them aside. She loosened the laces on her blouse and at the waist of her skirt and threw them toward her boots. Extending her hand toward Caol, she stepped into the pool to her ankles.

Caol dropped his hand to his side, frowning, as he scanned her chemise covered body. "Hmm," he murmured just before he flipped backward. His feet were the last part of him to disappear beneath the surface.

Sheridan grinned and tugged the kerchief from her head. Caol was certainly not a shy man. She looked down at her chemise and then scanned her surroundings for any prying eyes. Over these last weeks, Vali had appeared out of nowhere seemingly to just "walk along with you", he would say. From time to time, she had spotted the Island rebels standing high on a cliff when she was walking along the ocean's shore or leaning casually against a tree as she ventured to the dock to barter her wares with the trade boats. Spying on her, she was sure. Sheridan eyed the area a final time, then lifted the chemise over her head and dove into the water hole.

The cool water had only a moment to enfold her before Caol found her beneath the surface, deep in its depths. Silence embraced her, pounding at her ears, drawing her to him. Caol swam around her, softly caressing the back of her calves, her thighs. His hands skimmed across her belly and then over her hips, tantalizing her, luring her to him. When she reached for him, he shifted from her and spun around her again and again, stroking her thighs, a gentle brush at her hands and along her arms. When they surfaced for air, he was behind her hugging her to him, running his mouth, his tongue, along her neck, her shoulder, her ear.

"Tis best to stand together, you and I, to battle this problem."

And then, they were below the water again, plunging into its depths. Twirling, she wrapped herself around his body, clutching him around his shoulders, her legs around his waist. She swirled with him as they spun and whirled, danced and frolicked through the caresses of the water's ripples.

He was inside her when they emerged, when she and Caol tumbled onto the mossy shore, gasping for breath, grasping each other and twirled one more time to ecstasy.

Sheridan stood, looking down at her sleeping husband. She placed his plaid gently over him. His dark brown hair, still slightly damp, lay around his shoulders and a low murmur whispered through his lips. The high noon sun indicated that they had slept for some time.

She shook her head, scolding herself. She had not shared her story with Caol. He had smiled and she had fallen into his arms. A niggle of guilt tapped at her thoughts. All the promises he had made to her last night and this morn were stated in the heat of their lovemaking. Did he really mean all he said? Could she trust him with her most treasured secret? Would he really stand with her?

Sheridan brushed her hands over her skirt and blouse and tied her kerchief at the nape of her neck, fully dressed now. She pulled herself away, edging backward quietly to not disturb Caol. She walked around the boulder. All seemed deserted. She turned toward the sea and then looked back a final time. "So be it."

Sheridan ran to the cliff, pleasuring in the wind pushing against her and chasing away her uncertainty. She looked down and nodded once. Then, grasping her rope, she lowered herself over the cliff edge and began her descent to the shore, to the cave, to the ponies, to her Angel. To her peace.

Chapter Five

His wife had not come home. Caol stomped along the pathway, his steps in rhythm with his silent mantra—his wife had not come home. Twas the third time he had awakened without her. Irritating, it was. Another Island tradition? Strange, the ways of these Islanders.

Yesterday morn, he had awakened alone. Yesterday afternoon at the swimming hole, when he had opened his eyes to stare into that blue sky above and turned toward her—he growled low—she was gone, leaving him sleeping beneath his plaid. And this morn? She had not come home last night. He had fallen asleep waiting for her and she had not returned. He was equally irritated with himself and if he had been able, he might have given himself a kick in the arse. How could he have fallen asleep waiting for her? He had meant to go back into the night, searching. Yet he had sat down on the chair, contemplating his plan, and had fallen—his growl mounted to a short bellow—asleep!

Caol turned toward Alan's and Ferna's croft. Mayhap he would find Sheridan there. Yesterday, after he had awakened beside the swimming hole—alone— he had searched for her along the west side of the Island. He had wandered along the cliff and shore, even ventured into a few caves. No Sheridan. It had been twilight when he had taken a meal along the shore with a local fisherman. Later he had walked to his marriage croft, hoping to find her there and had— bloody hell!—nodded off.

As he stepped onto the trail that led to his in-laws' home, the yellowed ferns fluttering in the breeze hailed the message that summer was fast disappearing. He sneered at the plants, sure they were shaking their withered fronds, reminding him that he had been late coming to the Island. These problems could have been avoided if he had arrived in the spring as he had promised.

Alan sat outside the small croft, stitching a torn fishing net.

"I have lost my wife," Caol stated. "Is she inside then?" He stepped into the wee house, built of peat and stone. A window lined each of the four walls of the house, their shutters open, making the interior bright. Ferna sat before the hearth, a shallow hole dug into the dirt floor and edged with stones. A small fire burned, chasing away the chill of the morning. She was stitching a design into a piece of cloth—likely a future product to be bartered at the dock.

"Caol has lost our Sheridan." Alan followed Caol inside and spoke from the doorway.

"Mayhap an Island tradition? A hide-and-seek game, where a new husband must find his wife." Caol was striving to be calm, to take the edge off his voice, but he knew that his sarcasm had been detected when Ferna raised her eyes to him, brows furrowed and mouth puckered.

"How many years have you, Caol?" she asked.

"Seven and twenty."

"Well now, I do not think you are too big or too old to receive a clout across your ears."

"The next Laird of Rose Castle cannot have an addled brain, Ferna," Alan cautioned.

"Well then," Ferna concluded.

Caol flopped into the chair opposite Ferna. "Good morn to you both, Ferna, Alan." His eyes followed a single wisp of smoke that rose upward to the pointed roof. It escaped through the smoke hole. He rubbed his hands over his face. He had brought his sour mood into this house where only kindness had been shown to him over the years. "I apologize for my rude, abrupt behaviour." He looked at Alan. "My worry and concern for Sheridan has me befuddled and out of sorts." He scanned the small croft. "She is not here, then?"

"The last we saw of Sheridan was three days past when the door to your marriage croft was abruptly slammed in our faces, Caol." Ferna's mouth puckered again and her brows rose in accusation.

Heat stung Caol's face as he rubbed a finger across his brow. He was doing a damned good job of raising the pique of his in-laws. He strove to keep a smile from his face, remembering his wedding night. When he looked to Ferna to apologize, by Crivens, he was sure a twinkle of humour sat behind her eyes.

"How long has she been lost?" asked Alan.

Caol sat straighter, pleased with the question, a diversion from an awkward conversation. "Tis a strange way to begin a marriage, I say." Alan's narrowed eyes caused Caol to select his words carefully. "Hidden ponies? Vali will not allow me to leave the Island until the ponies are found. The ship comes by again in two weeks and I intend to be on it." Caol paused. "With Sheridan." He raised his eyebrows, looking between his in-laws as they exchanged a glance.

"I have been unable to speak with Sheridan about the situation. There is more to the story, so it seems." Caol stood, walked to a window and scanned the landscape. Heat spread across his face. Twas not that he had been unable to talk with Sheridan about the problem. Rather he had been unable to keep his hands off her in these first few days of their marriage. When the flush of his untruth had subsided, he turned back to Alan and Ferna, shaking his head. "Why would Vali demand she marry him as payment for the lost herd?"

Alan stepped closer to him. "Twas a way to protect her from the rebels, Caol. In late spring, Vali approached Sheridan wishing to court her. Around the same time, the rebels began to make trouble for Vali. He told me, he felt Sheridan needed his protection."

Caol refused to be waylaid by the man's piercing stare. "Protect her?" Caol puffed out his breath. "I found her running to hide from Vali just three days past." Caol shook his head again. "Protect her? She must know that her family, her people will help her, not threaten her."

Alan tugged his shoulders back and lifted his chin. "You insult us, Caol, when you insinuate our lack of help, lack of protection." He thumped his hand against his chest and looked at Ferna. "Sheridan is our daughter. We love her dear. We believed marriage to be a solution to keep her from harm's way."

Ferna leaned toward Caol, frowning, and laid the cloth she had been embroidering on her lap. "Vali the Younger harped about marriage to Sheridan most of the summer. We knew not the anguish the plan caused her." Ferna shook her head as she spoke. "We learned in these many weeks that Vali has taken more and more to alcohol. He started to threaten Sheridan, saying 'she is to blame for the death of the herd and she will marry him'. A few days past, he had returned to the Island from drinking on the ships and declared that he and Sheridan would wed." She snipped the end of a thread with her teeth and folded the embroidered cloth. "At first, we saw the marriage to Vali only for her good. But now? Nay! With Vali behaving so strangely, so aggressively?" Ferna placed it into a basket. "We think not."

Only for *her good*. The words resonated with Caol. This past spring, his foster sister, Bonnie, had been forced into a marriage *for her own good*. Indeed his sister had been most unhappy about the arrangement but it had been necessary to ensure her safety.

Caol inhaled deeply. "I apologize. Again. Alan, Ferna. It was wrong of me to suggest you have not protected her." Possibly he did need the clout across the ears that Ferna had suggested. "Thoughtless, it was."

Ferna rose and handed the basket to Alan. "You will take this stitching to the dock for trade, aye? You can barter for some koffie beans. Twould be a fine treat."

She smiled at her husband and then walked to Caol. "Sheridan keeps many of her thoughts inside. Looking back, I realize that Sheridan could never marry the man who slaughtered her beloved ponies." She raised her eyebrows, resting her hand on his arm. "This I know, Sheridan is ne'er too far away. You will find her."

Dear God! Caol ran his hands through his hair and bit the inside of his mouth to prevent himself from arguing with Ferna. He was bewildered at such a calm statement from Sheridan's mother. She should be as concerned as he. "Hmm," Caol muttered. "Sheridan could be injured or accosted by the rebels who are also seeking the ponies." Caol lifted both arms and then dropped them to his sides. "Am I the only one concerned for her safety?"

Ferna looked at Alan for a moment and then cocked her head, listening. Twas a whisper of wind that caressed the small hut. And if one listened carefully, the strains of a flute tremored in the distance.

"All is well," Ferna declared. "Listen. The Angel sings."

"Dear God," muttered Caol. The superstitions and traditions on this Island made him weary. How on earth did a mythical angel's singing declare that Sheridan was safe?

"Ferna!" Alan scolded, taking a step closer. "He is not one of us!"

Ferna studied Caol's face for a time. "I think he is," she concluded, nodding her head.

"Enough!" commanded Alan. He eyed Ferna, long and hard, then pushed past Caol and stood again at the door. "Caol! Accompany me to the dock."

As Ferna turned away to stir the hearth, Caol followed Alan from the croft. Already his father-in-law had stridden past the withered ferns and disappeared around a copse of gnarled trees, bent from the ancient winds that blew across the Island. Caol caught up to him at the top of the cliff trail that led to the shore where the Island's large trading dock stood. Trade ships from northern Europe anchored off shore of the Island. From the ships, sailors rowed skiffs laden with goods to the dock and bartered for Island goods. Twas a productive industry.

"Alan, I have never been to a place where superstitions and traditions are treasured more than here. Tis beginning to grate against me." Caol spoke to the back of Alan's head as he followed him down the rock strewn trail. "Sheridan is missing and I have not gathered any more information from you or Ferna that will point me in her direction." Alan's head bobbed up and down as he walked over a large rock in the middle of the path. The rock had been there for as long as Caol could remember. "If I hear one more word about that damned Angel . . . I do not understand why I am the only one who appears to be concerned for Sheridan's safety."

Abruptly, Alan stopped. Caol was sure he heard him curse under his breath. The older man surveyed the landscape below and then turned north away from the dock and strode down to the shore. Caol walked beside his silent father-in-law for a distance. Eventually the older man stopped beside a skiff. The small boat had been capsized, with its keel up, to keep the rains and ocean water from accumulating inside. He and Alan leaned against it, staring out to the ocean. Far out, a few large ships were anchored, gently swaying on the choppy waters.

"I met Ferna just that way." Alan pointed to the large ships. "Even though Vali Island is an isolated place, the ships from Rose Lands were the first to venture here, all those years ago." He smiled. "I was a young lad when I signed with Rose Castle to be a workman on its ships. When we sailed to this Island, Ferna was often at the shore. I was smitten. Took some getting used to living here amongst her people." He crossed his arms. "The De Ros ways, the mainlander ways." Alan flung his arm toward the south. "Even some of the other Islands follow Scottish traditions, aye? But here, tis Norse ways." He shrugged. "Our ways, Ferna's and mine, were different. But in time, indeed, our traditions blended."

"But, Alan, how can mine and Sheridan's traditions blend? I cannot accept the ludicrous belief of an Island Angel." He shook his head and turned to Alan. "Even the fisherman that I supped with last eve talked of the Angel. The sailors from the large ships tell him that Vali the Elder's fire still burns and glows. Indeed, they see it regularly." Caol looked skyward, shaking his head. Throughout windy and fog laden nights, Vali the Elder had burned a large fire at the northern point of the Island to warn ships of the rocky shoreline. "The fisherman claimed that the Angel of the Island burns the fire now. Surely, Alan, it cannot be. And yet, even Sheridan speaks of the Angel as if it were real."

Alan spoke softly. "This beloved Island. Its traditions and superstitions are all part of our Sheridan." Alan turned to Caol and narrowed his eyes. "As Ferna and I accepted each other's ways, our love deepened."

"But, I cannot—"

"Caol!"

Caol turned quickly to Alan's commanding tone.

"Are you listening, man? Perhaps a clout across your ears would help!" Alan inhaled deeply. When he spoke again his calm had returned. "Sometimes, Caol, you must listen more and talk less."

When Caol opened his mouth to rebuff Alan's rebuke, his father-in-law interjected. "Sheridan chose you. Vali offered for her but it was you she wanted."

"But, Alan—"

"Prove that you are worthy of her choice, Caol De Ros!" Alan turned toward the dock and marched away, gripping Ferna's basket of goods in his hand.

"Hmm," Caol breathed, rubbing his hand across the back of his neck. Alan's final words had been a clout across the ears and a kick in the arse. Never had he known Alan to be so critical. Caol had simply been looking for his wife, not seeking marital advice from her parents. Together he and Sheridan would work on their marriage once they were settled at Rose Castle with its familiar ways and its sane logic.

Caol pushed himself off the skiff and stood, stretching his neck to ease his tension. Why had Sheridan not come home? By God, he had to find her to ensure her safety.

Slowly he turned in a full circle and then stood tall, hands resting at his belt, legs apart, staring north. The ponies had often grazed and lived about the Island's northern point. Had she hidden them in that direction? And likely Sheridan would be with the ponies.

Caol strode along the same shore that he had taken upon his arrival to Vali Island three days past, hoping it would lead him to Sheridan . . . again.

Chapter Six

The tide was high and Sheridan was glad for it. The path along the seashore she would normally follow to get to her rope was hidden under the water. To scale the cliff wall would bring her to the top of it and to her wedding croft faster. In all truth, she was in no hurry to return to her croft.

Sheridan climbed an alternate route, the stone stairway carved into the rock's edge by ancestors past. The secret steps meandered upward to the top of the cliff. Twas a long route, these many steps, but it gave her time to determine what to say to Caol.

How did she explain to her husband why she had left him sleeping at the water hole and stayed away all night? She had only meant to visit with Angel a short time.

She wanted to tell her friend about her decision to share the secret—she planned to tell Caol about Angel. But when she had arrived yesterday, one of the ponies had appeared sick. Its head drooped low. Twas so uncharacteristic of that mare that Sheridan had been frightened by the sight. Had the pony caught the spring disease? She and Angel had tended to the mare throughout the night and by this morning the pony appeared well.

Sheridan shook her head as she climbed higher. She had already disappointed Caol by not explaining the full situation on the Island. But two days ago when Caol had found her descending the wall, she had been too anxious to fully describe the pernicious events. Had she purposefully chosen to not tell Caol about the ponies that day? She sighed in frustration. Twas difficult to find the words to explain why two hidden ponies had made her the target of Vali's determination to wed her, and the rebels' desire to accost her. In all truth, she had not shared fully. If she had spoken about the ponies, she would also have had to tell Caol about Angel.

As Sheridan rounded a corner of the rock staircase and began to ascend to the next level of steps, some pebbles rolled down the cliff wall. Startled, she looked up to the top of the cliff, scanning its edge. Strange that pebbles would fall, for at the top of the cliff edge gorse bushes grew. So thick were the bushes, twas near impossible for anything to penetrate the barrier.

And yet, had someone found this secret pathway? Hesitant to continue, Sheridan sat on a step for a time, waiting to see if more pebbles would tumble down.

She stared out to the sea, watching as the surf rolled toward the shore, its droning hum booming loudly each time it splashed against the rock wall. A ship had anchored far out on the ocean, its rowboats moving south toward the dock on the east side of the Island. Boats never ventured close to this shore, the Island's northern point, below Vali the Elder's resting place. This shoreline was too rocky, too shallow at low tide and the winds rounding the tip could be unpredictable. Twas a perfect location for her precious ponies to be hidden.

The morning air was nippy, the wind restless, and Sheridan pulled on her gloves and tugged her cape tightly about her. She placed her elbows on her knees, resting her chin on her hands. She desperately wanted to share her secret with Caol. *Come, come with me. Let me show you a part of myself you know nothing of.* The words seemed simple enough to say now, while she stared out to sea. It was just . . . Caol was a practical man, who did not embrace the mystical. To be sure, he did not appreciate the superstitions of her Island.

Sheridan rubbed her roiling stomach, then

traced a crimson butterfly embroidered on her cape with her finger, remembering how Caol, jokingly, had slammed the door in her people's faces. Oh, how he had failed to see the love and appreciation of those dear merry-makers during the wedding celebrations.

Rubbing her temples, she exhaled, her breath fluttering the bangs that peeked out beneath her hair band. Today, she planned to tell Caol about this Island's long kept secret. Would he be astounded? She rolled the word around on her tongue, then smiled. Aye, astounded. Such a skeptic, he was. Could she trust a skeptic with the knowledge of Angel?

Sheridan rose and looked above. All appeared peaceful except for some kittiwakes flying over, squawking at the ocean, anticipating the treasures the tide would wash in. She continued her climb, running her hand along the cliff wall as she mounted each step, remembering the night she had led the two mares down this long and arduous trek. She had tethered them together, one trailing the other and she leading, as they slowly and carefully, step by step, arrived at their hidden destination. The night had been dark and she had run her hand against this stone wall to guide her steps.

Arriving at the top of the cliff, she looked out on the ocean a final time. Twas a lofty location where she stood, the trail hidden well by the wall of gorse bushes.

They grew, bent and gnarled, to her waist and prevented anyone from seeing this secret passageway of steps. She walked along the edge for a distance and then stepped out, far from the pathway, far from her secret. Sheridan scanned the area. Possibly a small animal or a bird had skittered over the ground and scattered the pebbles that had rolled down the cliff's face.

Sheridan walked to a large boulder to which she always secured her rope when scaling the wall. The rope was still tethered to it and dangled over the cliff edge from its use, two days past, when she had met Caol on the seashore below. When it was not being used, she always coiled the rope and hid it in a hole beneath the boulder. She now grasped it and pulled, hand over hand.

Years ago, she had been given the rope by some sailors. Papa had allowed her to accompany him as he rowed out to one of the large ships that anchored offshore. On the ship, some sailors had hoisted her to sit aloft one of the booms. She had loved being so high, dangling above the vast sea, perched above the ship like a bird. They had given her a length of rope that day and she had since treasured it.

After, Papa had let her scale low cliff walls, never too high, and by and by, she had outgrown the sport. Twas when she had discovered that descending this cliff wall would be a shorter route to her Angel than the long walk down the steps, she had decided to add length to the rope. She had bartered at the dock for more rope and had woven the pieces together until finally it had grown long enough that her toes touched the seashore below.

Sheridan coiled the rope around her elbow and hand and then shoved her forearm through the centre of the twisted cable to carry it. Twas heavy and she used her other hand to help heave it around to place it in the hole.

She froze. Across the expansive rock plateau stood Geir, one of the rebels who spoke against Vali the Younger and who had threatened her throughout this summer. She had been ever so careful to avoid these rebellious men and mostly had stayed close to her parents and out of harm's way. But now, there stood Geir upon a rock incline on the far side of Vali the Elder's cairn, staring at her.

"I thank you, Sheridan, for showing me the way. I found the path just a short time ago." Twas his brittle laugh that made her stomach clench. "Surely, I thought, no sane person would dare take ponies down that cliff trek. But sure enough, there was dried horse shite at the top of the steps."

The churning in her stomach intensified as he pulled a dagger from his belt. But twas the cynical way he dusted the Elder's cairn with a scornful sneer and then leaned against it that made her lift her chin and narrow her eyes. Twas sacred ground that he stood on. He did not belong here, at the Elder's resting place.

"Then you stepped from the path. Only Sheridan, the woman who hangs from cliff walls, would dare such a feat." Geir pushed away from the cairn. "Twas our plan this day to search the north point for clues. I above, and some men below, searching along the shore for the treasured ponies."

Sheridan remained as still as the Elder's cairn, measuring Geir's intent as he took slow steps toward her. She was certain that he had not ventured down the steps yet. How could she make certain that this lout would never trek that path, or touch the ponies, or find the secret hiding place? The rope that she held over her arm felt her caress as she slowly released its end and allowed a length to unravel to her feet.

With his arm outstretched now, Geir continued to approach. "I will take that rope, Sheridan, and tie you securely before I venture down those steps."

Sheridan had only used her rope for practical purposes, for loving purposes, such as leading the ponies or scaling the cliff wall to visit her Angel. Never had her rope been used as a weapon. Her heart beat ever so fast and she held her breath for a moment to still her trembling as the man came closer and closer.

She could never outrun him and she could not physically prevent him from starting down the path. She had never before done what she was about to do. Would her plan work? She would only need a portion of the rope to tether this brutish thug and tie him so that she could run for help.

Sheridan threw the coiled cable upward, grasping tightly to its end and twirled it around the boulder several times to shorten its length. As the man rushed toward her, she ran toward the edge of the cliff and lowered herself over. Pulling the rope under her bottom, she tethered it tightly above her so that she sat on it as if it were a swing. Grasping the swing's handles tightly with her arms, she twisted the rope and tied a loop at the rope's end, coiled the remaining cable and held it ready. She waited, her pulse pounding and only found the courage to look up when tiny pebbles skittered down the rock wall, a few skipping off her nose.

Geir was there, looming over the cliff edge and holding a knife, readying to cut the rope from which she swung and see her fall to the shore, far below. Dead. She shivered. Likely she would be washed out to sea, never to be found. Surely her plan had to work.

Just as Geir knelt to sever her swing, Sheridan flung the looped rope high. It flared above his head and fell down around his body. She cinched it tightly as it snared him around the middle. And then she tugged, grasping the rope with all her strength and pulled him over the edge. The man's startled screech echoed off the rock wall as he fell past her. An abrupt spasm on the rope indicated he had fallen the length of it and now dangled far below her. She pulled a dagger from her boot and sawed. When the rope snapped, the man fell farther down the rock wall and landed on a moss-covered ledge that protruded from it.

Breathing deeply, she swiped at the tears trickling down her face. Tears of relief, tears of joy. So amazed was she that her plan had worked. She actually had tossed the brute onto the ledge below and managed to remain on her swing.

Sheridan scrambled up onto the cliff and peered down at Geir. From time to time, when she had descended this cliff to visit her Angel, she had rested on the very spot where the man now stood. Never would he be able to climb up or climb down from that ledge.

Geir had loosened the rope from around him now and stood, bellowing up at her. She narrowed her eyes, studying him. Since early spring, her father had insisted that she carry her daggers and hang her sword on her back. She supposed she might throw her daggers at him, but . . . She just could not bring herself to end the man's life. She shook her head as a memory of Vali slaughtering the ponies loomed about her. Or any life! All life was precious.

Geir appeared uninjured and scrambled about collecting arrows that had fallen from his quiver. When he pulled his bow and readied to shoot an arrow upward at her, Sheridan stepped away from the edge, a shiver skittering up her back. Her assailant would not hesitate to kill her if he could. She could not fathom how her death could be worth two ponies to the man.

Sheridan turned toward Vali the Elder's grave, scanning the area briefly. All appeared safe atop this cliff now. She would have to get help for the brute. She would find Vali and Papa too. And Caol, she would find him.

Geir's words niggled at her—*some men below searching along the shore*. An unsettling breeze wafted about and the strings of her headband fluttered, tapping about her head, heightening her alarm. If the men below followed the shoreline they might discover her ponies. And Angel! Only the high tide would prevent them from journeying to the north point. She nibbled at her bottom lip. She'd wait to get help. She had to make sure the ponies and Angel were hidden securely.

Sheridan turned again to the pathway and hurried down the steps.

Chapter Seven

The waters splashed about his boots, as Caol waded through the ebbing tide. The high surge had delayed his search considerably, forcing him to sit on top of a large boulder for a time, waiting for the waters to lower. Now with each step forward, his confidence grew that he was following the correct path to Sheridan. He was certain when three days past Sheridan had said she would hide in a cave, she had looked to the northern tip of the Island. Twas as if she had known precisely where she was going. The ponies were there and so was Sheridan!

The waters had receded enough to provide a narrow strip of shore to hike along. Walking in the shadows of the cliff wall prevented Vali's guards and the group of rebels from spying Caol from above. With each step, the surf washed away his footprints.

He was well hidden.

Caol's chuckle changed into a low growl. A

sneer marred his face. Well-hidden indeed. Just like his wife. In their three days of marriage, he had spent verra little time with her. Twas not easy to accept the truth—his wife did not quite trust him. He rubbed his chest. His vows to her had been heart-made. What had deterred her from believing him? Why had she even married him? She certainly was not seeking his protection if she could not trust him enough to reveal the secret location of the ponies.

"My wife is a mystery and I am a besotted fool," he murmured.

Indeed! Twas that very quality about Sheridan, a mysteriousness, entwined with her quiet nature that had caught his eye. Her dark eyes, appearing to hold unspoken secrets, had captured his attention, had drawn him to her. He had yearned to know what was hidden behind Sheridan's shy smile that teased him even now as he plodded along this narrow path. Caol kicked the water in frustration and then swiped at the droplets that splashed his face.

Twas not only his wife's lack of trust that left a bitter taste in his mouth. Neither did his in-laws trust him. The glances that passed between Sheridan's parents had not gone unnoticed. They knew something. Something that no one wanted to share with him.

Alan's words still stung. *He is not one of us.*

Caol sighed in exasperation. What must a man do to become one of them? From a very early age—four or five years—he had visited this Island with his father each summer. He had wandered the Island with Petter. From time to time, Vali had joined them in their summer adventures, if just to boss and bully them.

Damn Vali. The lying coward had tried to bully Sheridan into marriage and had refused to acknowledge it in their conversation yesterday. He wished that Petter were still living on the Island. The sensible son of Vali the Elder. Indeed, Petter would have been able to cast clarity over the situation. Yet there was no future for the second son of the Lord, here, on Vali Island. Petter had left years ago to work on the ships that sailed the North Sea.

Caol growled low again and looked out to the ocean. Twas as if he had been tossed out to sea and was struggling in the waters to stay afloat. Twas a murky place to exist.

The waterfall Caol had splashed through three days ago loomed before him. He pulled his leather cape closer around him and tugged his wide-brimmed hat lower on his brow. The high waters would force him to climb precariously behind the waterfall to the adjoining shore. He climbed atop a large boulder and stepped onto a ledge that jutted from the cliff wall. The water cascaded at his back and his nose bumped against the rock wall as he slid, step by step, sideways along the shelf.

Emerging on the other side, his stomach roiled and his throat tightened. He would willingly walk through a hundred waterfalls rather than climb the rock bluff looming before him. The tide was ebbing, yet it still floated high around the bend that meandered out into the ocean. How he wished he could swim that trek, or even wade around it like he had three days ago. But even with his excellent swimming abilities, he couldn't risk it. High tide brought undertows and hid jutting rocks. He would have to climb.

Caol inched his way upward, trying to not think about how much he hated heights. Yet his efforts failed and he stilled for a moment and strove to wipe the memory from his thoughts, but there it was. He, a young lad of five years, standing at the brink of a cliff looking down.

His clan had just laid his mother and infant sister to rest in a deep burial pit. Slowly each clan member had carried a stone to that pit to cover their bodies. When his turn came to place his rock, he had approached the site and angrily had thrown it into that dark pit. All these years later, he could still hear the jarring bang as it crashed onto the other stones. He had been so furious at his mother and infant sister for leaving him.

Then he had run. Run from the kirk gravesite, from the tears and sniffles of the others, from the droning words of the priest, from the truth—his mother was dead! Caol had finally come to a halt at the brink of a cliff. Looking over the edge, down into that deep abyss, it had appeared just like the pit where his mother lay. Dead! He had screamed that word. Dead! Indeed, he had thrown rocks over the cliff edge until he was exhausted. That lad of all those years ago had finally sat down and vomited over the edge—a final purge of his wretchedness, his loneliness. Even some of his anger.

Yet strangely, that day, the boy Caol had walked away from the cliff edge with a subtle fear of heights. As a man, Caol still did not understand this notion. Mayhap that is why he had taken to the water. He would rather swim around a rock wall than climb high and look down—down into that pit from so long ago.

Caol continued to move upward and when he dared look down once, he had to breathe deeply to ward off the vomit crawling up from his gut. In all truth, this rock bend was hardly high, yet it surely rattled him. Unlike his wife, who for as long as he could remember, had with exhilaration, thrown herself over cliff walls. "Hmm" A few years ago, he had been shocked to learn that she scaled high cliffs. He had demanded Sheridan, his friend, to stop such foolishness. He had finally received her promise when even Ferna and Alan had warned her about it.

Relief embraced Caol as he ventured down the other side and stepped onto the sandy shore. The daylight had passed into the afternoon and he pulled lunch from his backpack. He stood, scanning the area as he ate and drank. He still had not found his wife but he was sure she had looked to the far shore when she had spoken of hiding in a cave. The water had edged lower and it would take a few hours, along this path, to round the cliff point and find the cave. It had to be there and so was Sheridan. *Dear woman.* Warding off any thoughts of failing to find her, he stuffed the final crust of bread into his mouth.

A faint sound behind him and Caol turned his head sharply. "God Almighty," he bellowed as he scrambled to his right. An arrow landed in the very spot where he had just stood. Raising his eyes, he saw a man standing on a high ledge that jutted from the cliff. Twas the same wall, Sheridan's wall, she had scrambled down a few days past.

"You bloody fool," Caol sneered.

The man waved his arms, yelling. Yet the roar of the waves and the sheer height of the ledge from the ground prevented Caol from understanding what he said.

Caol scanned the shoreline. No Sheridan. Then he slowly raised his eyes to the top of the cliff. Was Sheridan above, wounded or . . . A grave fear snaked its way upward, readying to choke Caol's breath as he turned to the sea. Was the man one of the rebels who opposed Vali? Had Sheridan crossed this man's path? Had he harmed her and during high tide, thrown her over the cliff into the sea? "Was she dea—?"

Caol turned back to the rock wall, biting down hard on his tongue refusing to release that word. Dear God, please! Let it not be so. But twas no good to see that man on Sheridan's wall. There was no rope dangling from the cliff edge so how in hell had he landed there? Caol refused to venture any deeper into those thoughts. With the taste of blood on his tongue, anger surged through him. The man would pay for any harm he had brought to Sheridan. For now, he would remain a captive on that ledge.

His heart pounding even harder than when he had ventured over the rock bend a short while ago, propelled Caol forward. Grabbing his backpack he ran along the shore toward the northern point. He had to find Sheridan . . . alive!

Twilight was just a breath away. The western horizon shone in the final oranges and pinks of light's farewell. Caol was sure he was closing in on the cave and Sheridan.

The shore meandered along the high cliff wall, veering inward to the northernmost point of the Island. He had studied the wall along his trek and after some time, had spied this cove that seemed to disappear into a narrow alleyway. Caol stilled for moment, sniffing the wind that tunnelled through the narrow passageway, smacking him before it passed on to the sea. Was it demons or friendly spirits that beckoned him to enter? He breathed deeply, refusing the urge to run through this tunnel bellowing for Sheridan. Rather, he settled a hand on the hilt of a dagger secured at his belt and stepped forward.

Caol followed the narrow path shadowed by rock walls looming so high that when he looked up he could not see where the walls ended and the sky began. He ducked quickly as a flock of starlings swooshed past him. Twas odd this particular bird flew here, near to these wind-blown cliffs.

After a time, the passageway widened and the gloomy shadows disappeared. Caol blinked and rubbed his eyes to ensure that what he saw was true. Before him, lay a deep valley covered in grass. Caol smiled for he was sure he saw, even in the meagre light, two ponies grazing in the distance.

Never, in all the years that he had visited this Island, exploring, had he heard a word about this place. This valley was encircled by cliff walls which barred any view of the ocean. Twas a spot so well hidden few would ever spy the entranceway and find this haven.

Bitterness rimmed the edges of Caol's smile. He knew Sheridan was close by, that he was closing in and would soon find her. He felt it. Indeed, she was well. Yet he rubbed his chest to ease away an unseen wound. What had prevented Sheridan from sharing this secret with him?

Caol walked around a large boulder and stood before a rock staircase that led upward to the top of the cliff or downward toward the shore. Sheridan had spoken of a cave and likely it would be closer to the water. Following the stairs downward he trekked along a trail that was shadowed by a rocky bend. A bitter chuckle rippled from him for there it was, a small arched hole in the side of the rock wall. The cave.

No longer did Caol walk thoughtfully along the trek but strode toward the cave, bending low to pull his frame through the entranceway. He stood tall again and pushed forward toward a faint light that flickered far down the passage way. He stomped along the pathway, his steps in rhythm to his silent mantra—*time to share your secrets, Sheridan. Time to share your secrets.*

Rounding a corner, Caol stopped abruptly,

staring into a conical rock cavern that rose up to an open hole at its peak where moonlight shone through. He gulped, swallowing his sour mood. Where was his wife? He stood taller, hands at his belt, legs spread, refusing to acknowledge the cold shiver that ran along his spine. Mayhap twas demons that had beckoned him at the narrow passageway and now wafted about him, for an eerie figure, robed in a dark hooded cape, sat before a fire. Wisps of smoke encircled the cave, rising up and escaping through the hole. Twas a disturbing sight.

He must have made a sound, although he was sure his throat had tightened and he could not draw air, for the figure turned its head toward him. Twas a ghost that rose from its seat and floated slowly toward him, amidst the smoke and hazy light of the moon. Sweat beaded Caol's brow and his hands tightened at his belt as the ghost peered out at him from beneath its hood. Its colourless face was framed with hair as white as the foam of the ocean. Its eyes were as pale as the smoke that rose up to the hole and glittered with a faint red sheen. Twas all he could see of the apparition, for whatever other body parts it had were covered in that dark hooded cloak.

Caol stumbled backward as the spirit came closer and closer. "J—, Jesu," he stuttered, his hand instinctively rising to touch his forehead, his chest and both shoulders. "Jesu!" he bellowed, making the sign of the cross again, before he closed his eyes and lifted his arms to protect himself, certain that the echoed response would bring down the rocks around him.

Silence! Indeed, the place was so muted that he could count the beats of his heart. Caol drew a deep breath, lowering his arms, and peered again into the cavern. The spectre stood a few feet from him, staring. Caol pushed himself back against the rock wall, slithering down onto a boulder. How did one contend with a ghost?

A soft patter of footsteps, a flash of movement and his wife popped her head out from behind the spectre. Fear sat at the edges of her eyes.

"Sheridan," he barely whispered.

"Caol." There was relief in her voice. "I am so glad it is you." She stepped beside the figure and extended her hand toward him. "Please Caol. Don't be afraid. Tis the Angel of the Island."

Chapter Eight

The night was dark. The moon and stars had retreated behind the heavy clouds. Angel had slipped away to the valley to tend to the ponies. Angel's introduction to Caol had been . . . silent. Caol had just stared at Angel until she had silently slipped away. Sheridan sighed as Angel's music floated to her. She imagined the ponies standing close to Angel as she played her flute.

After Angel had left, Sheridan had taken a silent Caol by the hand and led him outside through the back entrance of the cave. This spot was a quiet and private place where her words would be heard by no one but Caol.

Sheridan threw a chunk of dried peat into the firepit and looked across the flames to where Caol sat on the sandy ground. He stared up at the rock that loomed beside him, watching as the fire snapped higher, causing the light to dance up the wall and flare into the night sky.

"Indeed the Elder's fire does burn."

"Pardon, Caol?" Sheridan leaned closer to the fire unsure of what Caol had muttered.

Caol turned an intense gaze to her, his eyes holding hers for a time. Then he shook his head and looked again, upward, to the rock wall.

Sheridan too looked up at the wall that sheltered this spot from heavy winds and high tides. The dancing light from the fire often shone above the stone wall. She had heard the sailors at the dock speak about Vali the Elder's fire and how it still burned. Is this what Caol had muttered about?

Behind Sheridan was the small back entrance to the cave through which she and Caol had just exited. A heavy leather curtain was its door. A rock ledge protruded over it so that on rainy days she and Angel could sit under it and remain dry. She reached for the basket of yarns atop the ledge. She pulled out her knitting and found some comfort in the rhythm of the needles as they clicked across a line of stitches.

"Angel and I work together here to create leggings, hats and scarves to barter at the dock." The needles clicked faster as her words poured out. "I knit and Angel embroiders the delicate shapes of birds, flowers and butterflies on them. These items are quite popular at the dock."

What was she doing, prattling on like a child?

She had spent these early days of her marriage mostly avoiding Caol, unsure of how to share this conversation with him. No longer could she use excuses to not go home—the pony was well and Angel had agreed to share the secret with Caol. And as for the knitting . . . Sheridan set it back into the basket. Twas now time to summon her courage and speak her truth. Sheridan pulled her knees to her chest and traced an embroidered flower at the hem of her skirt with her finger, organized her thoughts, and then looked again at her husband.

When Caol slid his eyes to her, her heart leapt and a warmth radiated across her breast. Would she ever find the courage to tell Caol how deeply she cared for him? That she had counted the days until his return to her Island each summer? That she admired his commitment to his clan, so thrilled she was to be part of his people now? The wildness in his spirit sent her heart soaring and called her to follow him. Oh, how she yearned to sit beside him now, to caress the frown from his face and see him smile again. But when Caol swiped his hat from his head and tossed it at his feet, her throat tightened. He was angry!

"I could not tell Vali the Younger where I had hidden the ponies for then Angel would have been discovered." At this moment, she was relieved that

Caol had found this place. He could help her deliver the ponies to Vali tomorrow. "The ponies are well and healthy and can be returned to Vali. But first, he must promise not to harm them." Her heart tightened with images of Vali slaughtering the sick ponies. Would she ever be able to forgive him?

Caol gave the slightest of nods. Twas strange to see him so still and quiet, for he was mostly a boisterous man, constantly active. An adventurer who loved to tell stories rather than listen to them. This Caol, this fretting man who sat across from her, was new and it forced her to order her words in her head and determine how to begin her tale. Oh, how she hoped he would believe the tale she would share and hold it as dearly as she.

"Only Vali the Elder, Mama and Papa and I know of Angel. An oath of silence had been given to ensure the woman's safety." She slid her hand up her arm to ward off the chill and found another embroidered flower on her sleeve to trace. "We were unable to share Angel with you, with others, for she lives in danger."

Caol moved his head slightly as if signaling her to continue.

"Six years old, I was, when I met Angel. Tis a vague memory, it is, but I recall I had followed the ponies to the northern tip of the Island that day."

Sheridan looked up into the dark sky and smiled, envisioning the time so long ago when she met her dear friend, Angel. "Twas a sunny day, windy, and my hair swept across my face as I watched the ponies grazing. When I pushed the hair from my eyes there was Vali the Elder, stepping around the thicket of gorse that grows along the edge of the cliff point." She looked again to Caol. "Surprised, the Elder was, to see me standing there. By chance, without meaning to, he had just revealed to me the secret passage way, a flight of rock steps that led to Angel's house." Sheridan extended her arm, "Here, to this place."

When Caol pushed his hands through his hair and cleared his throat, Sheridan hurried on. "You will listen, Caol." She was determined to finish her story before her husband started asking questions. She knew he would have many.

"When I looked behind the gorse bushes, from where the Elder had come, there I saw a set of stairs. The Elder explained they were ancient rock stairs used in the past by fishermen to carry their catch from the shore to above." Sheridan pointed upward. "To the cliff top. The steps had fallen into disuse, Vali the Elder explained, when he was a lad. The waters around this point are too rough and unpredictable for the fishermen to bring their boats and their catch to shore safely. It was then that the Island folk decided to build a large dock on the eastern shore."

The breeze wafted about and Sheridan moved a bit closer to the fire. If only Caol would come closer and settle beside her to chase away the chill that was beginning to take hold of her heart. But he only raised his brows when she extended her hands to the fire. She wondered if possibly this man who had vowed to be the keeper of her heart was having second thoughts about his promise?

"Vali the Elder tried to shoo me away from the rock stairs but I could not be deterred. I started down those steps and the Elder stayed close behind urging me to come back. Twas a long way down to this shore but I could not resist following that trail. Like a treasure hunt, it was. Here is where I met Angel. She stood along the shore with the late afternoon sun shimmering at her back. And she did shimmer, Caol. Dressed in white, the sun rays causing a lovely glow about her. She became my new friend."

With eyes dark and brooding, Caol studied her for a time, looked beyond to the entryway and then raised his eyes to the wall. He leaned a bit closer, across the fire, to her, and she allowed him to speak, if but a reward for coming closer. "Who is she? This . . . this Angel?"

"Tis a woman, the Elder told me, washed to shore many years past. She speaks not. Mute, she is.

Vali the Elder found her there, along the shore, almost dead and has cared for her since those days. She is most happy here amongst the rocks and sand. Never will she venture above to join our people, for she is hiding from . . ." Sheridan shrugged. "I know not. Only in darkness does she roam above to tend to the ponies." Sheridan swallowed the sorrowful lump in her throat. "When the ponies still lived."

Caol exhaled, making the flames flicker. "And Alan and Ferna? What are their thoughts about the woman?"

"Since that time, I have visited Angel often and she plays her flute to let my parents know that all is well. When Mama hears the music, she says 'the Angel sings'." Sheridan moved her head closer to Caol to whisper. "But Angel is a secret. No one is to know, for the Elder always said that danger surrounded her. Tis why she does not join our people, to live above."

"And from where did this woman come? This . . . this . . ." Caol cleared his throat as if to force the words out. "This Angel of the Island?"

Sheridan raised her chin and straightened her shoulders, refusing to be deterred from Caol's hint of sarcasm. "Vali the Elder believed she was sent by the gods from the otherworld, to watch over the Island." Sheridan raised her eyebrows in anticipation of Caol's disapproval of this superstition, but he simply stared back at her.

"But you, Sheridan, what do you believe?"

"To me, when I see her standing in the light of the moon, bright and shimmering, she seems mystical, to be sure. I know not from where she has come. From the sea? From the heavens? When I was a child, Papa told me stories of bright mystical beings. And so I call her Angel."

Caol rose from the ground and stood for a time, silent. "I have not believed in ghosts until this eve, Sheridan." His words trembled upon the gentle breeze and he looked up to the rock wall a final time, then turned and walked away.

She watched Caol stride into the darkness of the night, to walk along the distant shore, surrounded by the rhythmic sound of the waves. A final shadowy glimmer from his scabbard bade her farewell.

Melancholy crept into Sheridan's heart. He had left her here alone without any words of encouragement. She could only blame herself. She should have shared this secret when he had found her at the bottom of the cliff wall. Instead, gone was his good humour. And gone was her peace this place always provided. Her heart ached with grief.

Sheridan stood and threw a chunk of peat onto the fire. Flicking the leather curtain aside, she reached in and lifted some blankets from a small bench. She spread a blanket on the sandy ground close to the fire and lay upon it, pulling the other blanket over her. She rolled onto her side, pulling her knees up to her belly. She was tired. Maybe the morning would shed more light onto this predicament.

The warmth at her back chased the chill away and a hand rubbed her shoulder, caressing her, ever so gently, along her arm, to her waist, her hip. It tugged at her knees, pulling them down alongside his and now legs entangled with her own. "We will take the ponies to Vali on the morrow. Together." He raised her hand caressing it with his lips. "Your Angel will remain our secret." He tucked her hand beneath the blanket. "All will be well." Peace enfolded her.

Twas a good dream.

Chapter Nine

Caol opened his eyes and stared into the white mist floating in the small rock alcove where he lay with Sheridan. He smiled as he caressed his wife's back, so pleased he was that on this fourth morning of marriage she was actually lying beside him.

Sheridan slept, facing him with her head tucked down so that it rested on her hands. Her hair tumbled over her brow, a rich display of brown curls and as dark as the rivers and streams he had swum in as a boy. Indeed. She was as mysterious as those waters that meandered through the landscape at Rose Castle. Caol softly caressed a single curl with his finger. The blond tip of each curl was still on display, lightened by the summer sun. As long as he had known Sheridan, she had always worn her hair just past her shoulders, often pulled back with a kerchief tied at the nape of her neck. This morn, a hairband, intricately woven and embroidered with delicate flowers, lay askew amongst the curls. Sheridan moved her head in her sleep. Behind her closed lids were dark brown eyes with golden flecks, similar to the colour of the golden freckles that splashed across her nose and were painted under each eye.

Caol stared up into the white mist again and shook his head, thinking of last eve. Surprise mixed with anger and disappointment made a strange concoction of emotion. Astounded? Aye, astounded he had been when he had discovered Sheridan with the Angel of the Island.

As much as he was disappointed and even angry that Angel's story had never been shared, he could not be too surprised that it had been secreted away. After Sheridan had told the strange tale and he walked along the shore, he acknowledged that his people at Rose Castle had held his foster sister's secret close to their hearts, to protect her and to keep her safe. Even Vali the Younger had been surprised to learn that Bonnie was his foster sister rather than his biological sister. So surprised Vali was, he had even spewed his drink.

The sincerity of Sheridan's explanation about Angel convinced him that his wife, her parents and Vali the Elder had kept the secret for the same reasons as Rose Castle had—to protect Angel and to keep her safe.

When he had returned to her, Sheridan had fallen asleep, shivering under a single blanket. He had pulled her into his arms, this dear woman whom he had vowed to protect, to stand by, to fight for. As he had caressed the chill away, he had made another vow to her—*All will be well.*

Twas this vow that tangled with him now and nudged him from their bed, here, on the sand. He had to investigate Sheridan's strange tale, determine how to return the ponies and speak with Alan and Ferna about Angel's future. Soon Sheridan and he would be leaving the Island for Rose Castle and Angel would remain here, requiring help and even friendship.

Caol turned again to his wife. How he desired to remain in this place for a time, awaken Sheridan and invite her to love with him. Yet he could not. He gingerly attempted to crawl out from under the covers of their bed. Sheridan was a slight woman and was easily shifted as he pulled his arm from under her and stood. Twas a chilly morn and he tucked his woolen wrap closer about his sleeping wife. Twas a lovely picture, his wife covered in his plaid that displayed the colours of his clan.

Caol pulled on his woolen leggings beneath his tunic and donned his leather cape. Strapping his sword at his back, he started off. He would use this early morning opportunity to explore this place.

Caol held his skepticism tight to his chest, somewhat ashamed that it still lingered there. Surely he believed Sheridan's story, yet somehow he hoped it was all a dream—the Angel, the stairs, the music.

His stomach tightened as he pushed aside the heavy leather curtain and walked into Angel's rock cave, unsure of what, or whom, he would encounter. Twas an amazing place in the light of day. Across the space, wooden cupboards, suitable for a large ship, were positioned on either side of the cave's main entrance. A door was hinged between them, now closed. It must have been open last night, for he was sure he had walked down the path and into the cave unimpeded. Shelves were positioned on the walls and held a few wooden bowls, various pewter containers and several baskets with coloured yarns peeking above the rims. A hearth sat in the middle of the cave, and an iron pot held by a metal tripod hung over it. The smoke hole above, curtained with a fisherman's net to prevent small animals from entering, allowed the smoke to escape and the sunlight to enter. A wooden barrel stood close to the hearth, likely used to collect the rain that fell through the smoke hole. A table with two chairs was positioned in one area. Along the far wall, a stuffed cushion lay across a narrow rock ledge with a blanket neatly folded at one end.

But twas the small embroidered hangings

tacked on the walls, intricately stitched with scenes of nature that held his attention for a time. He studied each hanging carefully, recognizing the designs to be similar to the scenes embroidered on Sheridan's clothing. Twas a mystical place and his curiosity urged him to move about the room, touching the chairs, the shelves, even the cushion on the bed and, finally, one of the cloth hangings, simply to convince him that the place was real.

Twas real. Life lived here. He walked to the door and ran a hand along its frame and then grasped the cupboards on either side, attempting to shake them. Indeed, they were firmly secured. How on earth had these pieces of furniture come to be here? Vali the Elder had been a fine craftsman and he had to wonder about the Elder's part in the making of this place.

Caol knew he must make the most of this early daytime and hurry along. Sheridan liked to wake early but he wished to explore on his own without another impeding or directing his discoveries. He opened the door and followed the same pathway he had journeyed along the night before.

Turning the corner, Caol was sure his heart slammed into his ribs. The mystical creature that had scared the breath from him last eve stood before him. But in the light of day, twas no creature, but a woman who stared back at him. Only when Angel lifted the bucket she carried, dipped a wooden ladle into it and offered him a drink of the water, did he move. He narrowed his eyes, studying her carefully as he lifted the ladle to his mouth.

Angel's skin was as pale as the mist that welcomed the early morn. Thick white tresses spilled around the woman's face. She stared at him with eyes dimly coloured with blue and strangely rimmed in red. Never had he seen a person so pale—nay, so colourless. The woman wore the same dark cape as the night before, the hood pulled low on her brow. Scenes similar to those stitched on the wall hangings in the cave and on Sheridan's clothing were intricately embroidered along the edges of her cape.

"My thanks," Caol whispered as he bowed his head slightly and she accepted the wooden ladle with a smile. Although looking a bit closer, he was sure he saw a veiled attempt by her to withhold laughter. He could think of nothing but his frightened scream last eve that could have amused her. Twas good the woman could not speak and refused to roam above, so that no one would ever hear the tale of his first encounter with a ghost. She handed him a small leather bundle, tapped her hand to her mouth to indicate it was food, and then silently walked along the path to her rock house.

As Caol continued upward along the rocky trail,

his heart positioned itself rightly in his chest again. Indeed Sheridan's Angel was a startling sight. Yet in a peculiar sort of way, she was strikingly beautiful. "Hmm," he muttered. "Twas no Angel from the netherworld, but a person."

Caol stopped to look back one last time but the white woman had disappeared around the bend. For certain, the woman held many secrets and he looked forward to questioning Sheridan further about her Angel. Indeed, after listening to Sheridan's story about this woman, he had been most perplexed. As he had wandered off to walk last eve alone along the shore, he had gazed into the dark night and had listened to the rhythmic boom of the waves and wondered. Twenty years past, his foster sister Bonnie had been found at the door of an old woman's hut. Could it be possible that the Angel of the Island and Bonnie shared a common thread? Both had been secreted away all those years ago. He would discuss this idea with his father, Justus De Ros, when he and Sheridan finally arrived at Rose Castle.

Following the pathway, Caol eventually passed the juncture through which he had discovered the trail last eve. He ascended the steps, finally arriving at the secret passageway. Looking up, he realized the magnitude of his task. It would take him some time to reach the top but he patted the cliff's stone wall, ensuring that it was real. Twas real. And he began his ascent.

The trail did not meander into the rocky mountain but sat along the edge of the wall. It would be a treacherous plunge over the edge, but gorse and other vegetation acted as a barrier to prevent such a tumble. The foliage grew tall enough to block a seafarer's view of the steps from a ship, even if using a powerful spyglass to scan this distant horizon.

Higher Caol climbed, following the trail as it snaked along the face of the cliff. Stopping for a moment, he leaned against the wall and carefully peered over the side. Nausea rolled over him. His legs felt weak and twas not from this arduous climb. "Too high," he muttered as he stared down at the sea and the shore far below.

Caol determined he was about half-way in his journey. Mayhap food might calm his roiling stomach. He pulled the leather bundle that Angel had given him from a fold in his cape and opened it. Salted crab meat tumbled from the package and he sat on a step, looking down at the trek of stairs which he had just climbed. An image of his dead mother and infant sister wafted about him. "Hmm," Caol growled and turned in his seat to look up at the rock stairs he still had to climb.

Caol was now the same age—seven and twenty

years—as his father had been when he had lost his first wife, Caol's mother. Three years later, his father had taken Brianna MacEwen to marry. In time, Lady Brianna had become the mother that Caol had lost. Yet the image of his dead mother and infant sister in their burial pit had been seared into his mind, as real now as on the day his clan had buried them. As real as this cliff step he was sitting on.

Enough!

These meandering thoughts never led anywhere other than to sad memories of long ago. Caol rose, tucked away the leather bundle and steadily marched up the rock steps.

A final step, and Caol stood at the top of the cliff. Gnarled gorse bushes bordered a path to his left and he followed it, soon stepping from behind the barrier. Sheridan's story proved to be true, for here he stood at the northern tip of the Island, close to the Elder's burial cairn. Over the years, rarely had he explored this area of the Island, a rocky plateau that had been the favourite spot of the ponies. Rather, Sheridan, he, and Petter—even Vali had followed along at times—had wandered the shores and often rowed the skiffs along the coastline at low tide, searching for an evening meal of fish to take to Ferna. There was many an argument about who had caught the largest trout along the eastern coastal waters and lochs of the Island.

Caol turned and looked out to sea, wondering how Iain Campbell fared. A surge of anger speared from his gut and he breathed deeply to defuse it. He had unfinished business with Vali the Younger about the man's dealings with Campbell. He had words for Vali and he would speak them when he and Sheridan returned the ponies later this day.

His wife would be awake and likely wondering where he had ventured. Would her Angel be able to explain the direction he had hiked? He hoped Sheridan would remain at the cave until he returned, although his gut spoke skepticism on that thought. For the last four days, rarely had his wife been where he had hoped. Yet when he had crawled into their makeshift bed last night and whispered his thoughts of returning the ponies together, Sheridan had appeared to agree, turning to him and snuggling in his arms. Together they would ensure that the journey up the rock steps with the ponies would be safely accomplished.

Caol ventured closer to the cliff edge. "Sheridan's wall," he muttered. Indeed it was the verra cliff that she had descended four days ago when he had met her on the shore below.

He wondered how the man fared who stood on the ledge of this cliff wall. Caol's stomach roiled and he placed his hand on a large boulder, readying to peer down at the man. His foot struck something on the ground. Looking down, a rope lay tossed about the ground and partly wrapped around the boulder.

"Sheridan's rope!"

Snatching it up, he pulled a dagger from his boot. Damn it, he would get rid of it. Cut it to pieces! Destroy it!

"Bloody hell". He could not! Twas this very thread of wildness in Sheridan that matched his own and had drawn him to her throughout the years. He tossed the rope to the ground. He would speak to her and, once and for all, together they could determine what to do with the rope. "That damned, bloody rope!"

Caol shoved his dagger back into its sheath and scanned the shore below. The tide was creeping in, its rivulets slithering around the rocks and creating intricate patterns on the sand. A sudden movement on the shore, and he took a step closer to the cliff edge. The two ponies raced along the beach, necks extended, heads low to the ground, their manes and tails fluttering in the wind. And Sheridan ran after them! Was she returning the ponies? Without him? Surely she realized that the creeping waters would overtake them all if she didn't get to higher ground.

His body tightened in alarm. From the opposite direction along the shore, three men walked, nay stalked, toward Sheridan. Another step sent gravel tumbling over the cliff edge. Caol spied the man standing on the moss covered ledge below, holding his bow with the arrow aimed directly at Sheridan.

"Sheridan!" Caol bellowed.

Suddenly the man on the ledge fell to his knees, then tumbled down, falling hard onto the ground below and lay motionless. An arrow jutted from the man's back. Caol turned his head sharply. Vali the Younger stood tall on the edge of the cliff, some twenty yards away, still holding his bow high.

For certain, Caol knew his dear wife would be the next one to die. Vali the Younger's arrows could not reach the men on the shore who were steadily closing in on Sheridan. And never would Caol reach her if he followed his steps back down the rock stairs.

Sheridan's rope! He eyed it lying there on the ground. "Bloody, bloody hell," he moaned. Fear dampened his forehead and weakened his legs. Twas the only way down. His stomach threatened to spew the contents of his lunch at the thought of the sheer height of the cliff.

I pledge my oath that I will stand with you, fight for you and protect you, Sheridan, until our days are no more.

Caol nodded, closed his eyes tamping his fears to naught. He slid his eyes to Sheridan's rope and, bending down with steady hands, he grasped it.

He flung the rope high, unwrapping it from around the boulder and then tugged on it a few times. Tightening his grip, he lowered himself over the cliff edge, into the void below, crossed his ankles around the rope, and hurled himself down along the cliff wall. Sheridan's word, "expeditious", whispered at his ear.

Even before his feet touched the ground, Caol disentangled himself from the rope, tumbled onto the sand and then ran toward his dear wife. He drew his sword, measuring the distance to place himself between his wife and the approaching assailants. He splashed through the ankle-deep water when Sheridan suddenly saw the men approaching. One drew an arrow, but Caol was surprised to see him aim it toward a spot beyond Sheridan. He turned to where the arrow was pointing, the white woman walked into view.

"Angel!" Sheridan screamed and at that very moment the man let fly the arrow.

"Nay! Sheri—"

As Sheridan flung herself on top of Angel, Caol stepped into the arrow's path. It shoved him to the ground, a fiery convulsion throbbing across his back and taking his breath from him. He inhaled deeply, demanding himself to focus, to keep an eye on his wife.

Sheridan huddled over her Angel. Safe. He was sure his wife was safe.

The thought embraced him, gently, softly, as a grey veil, cold it was, settled over him. His eyes closed, his energy slipping away, logic and strategy long gone. Twas not how he had thought this would end.

His head dropped into the shallow water. He plunged again over the rock wall, into darkness, into the bottomless pit.

Chapter Ten

Caol lay unconscious in the rowboat, his body spread out on the bottom boards of the vessel. Sheridan held his head in her lap and applied pressure to the wound at his shoulder, trying to stanch the bleeding. She and Angel had torn material from their clothes and wrapped the wound but twas to no avail. In desperation, Sheridan snatched her kerchief and pressed it against the injury.

She closed her eyes to prevent any tears from seeping out as Vali the Younger steadily rowed the boat toward shore. The terrifying scene wound itself eerily through her mind, intensifying the trembling that had overtaken her.

Vali had followed Caol down the rope. As Caol stood between her and the assailants, Vali, with his bow and in rapid succession, pierced two of the men on the beach. Now they lay dead, alongside Geir, on the shore. The fourth man had run into a cave deep in the cliff wall. Remembering the speed at which Caol had come down that cliff caused her stomach to churn. Even she would never have tried to descend a wall at such a lightning-speed.

Vali had clipped the shaft of the arrow that had pierced Caol. But the tip of the arrow was deeply embedded in Caol's upper back. She, Angel and Vali had rolled Caol onto his cape and with great effort carefully lifted him into the rowboat. Vali had directed Angel to take the ponies to higher ground before the tide overtook them. Then Vali had rowed the skiff out to sea, around the rock bend and steadily toward the cliff path.

Caol's wedding night promise wafted about her. *Forever the keeper of your heart, Sheridan.* Is this what he had meant? Taking an arrow for her? Protecting her? Twas a heroic yet deathly choice.

Sheridan laid her forehead against Caol's, caressing his face, stroking his hands. "Live, Caol. I beg you to live."

The bellow of Vali's sounding-horn jarred Sheridan from her thoughts. Twas a single blast meant to beckon all men on the central eastern shore to emergency. The skiff touched ground and Vali jumped into the water, knee-deep, and pulled the small vessel higher to the shore. Several men ran down the cliff pathway and, spying them, hurried along the shore.

Papa was the first to arrive, demanding answers as he ran along the shore. "Sheridan what is it? Vali answer me." Coming to an abrupt stop, he stared into the boat. "Dear God." He stepped into the shallows to touch Caol's forehead and his hand. He leaned closer and glanced at the wound. "Dear God," he whispered again and then moved to the far side of the skiff to allow room for the other men to gather.

So breathless, was Sheridan, her words refused to form. "P. . . Pa . . . the . . . they found us, Papa. Everyone found us." She sat straighter in the boat, hands on either side of Caol's head. "We must get him to Mama." She scanned the men's faces, imploring them to action. "Quick. Run and ready Ferna."

Vali nodded to one of the guards who turned and ran back along the path from where he had just come.

"We will lift on my signal," Vali directed. Each man stepped forward and grasped onto Caol's cape. Vali nodded. Carefully, and with a few grunts, lifeless Caol was lifted in the sling and placed on the shore.

"Bloody hell," Caol muttered, his eyes opened and then rolled back into his head.

Again Vali directed. "On my signal, we will turn him onto his stomach."

Caol's face shoved heavily into the sandy beach as they rolled him over. "Have you no mercy?" Caol grunted into the earth.

Vali kneeled by Caol, and looked at the blood seeping through his tunic. "We give you all the mercy required to keep you alive." He pulled Caol's cape higher so that his face rested now on the softness of the cured leather.

The endearment lifted Sheridan's spirits. Caol and Vali, along with Vali's younger brother Petter, were like brothers, boys grown to men, who had played and worked together on this Island for a fortnight every summer for as long as she could remember. The scene at Vali the Elder's resting place yesterday had spoken of strife between the two men. Perhaps the healing of their conflict had already begun but now urgency was required to tend to Caol.

Vali rose from the sand and glanced at Sheridan and then to the skiff. "You will collect his weapons, Sheridan." For a moment, he looked out to the ocean and then turned to Alan. "'Tis best, Alan, if you row to the north shore, just past the waterfall, to determine if all is well." Next Vali turned to the men. "He will be carried to Ferna. Keep the cape as taut as possible. We will step in unison to ease the jarring." He took a deep breath, nodded once, then together with the men, leaned down and grasped a corner of the cape.

As the group of men walked along the shore to

the pathway, one guard droned a count to ensure a steady march. Twas like a dirge being sung and Sheridan could not help but think it a burial procession. Her dear husband was the corpse.

Enough! Such dark thoughts would not take care of the task at hand.

"Sheridan!"

Startled, she turned to her father's voice.

He stood holding Caol's sheathed sword out to her. "Your words make me think that perhaps our Angel has been discovered."

"Aye, Papa. The ponies escaped this morn and ventured out onto the shore. And the rebels were also at that shore, Papa. To be sure, they had rowed this boat around the rock bluff looking for the ponies." She turned back to watch the men. They were nearing the pathway that would lead them to the top of the cliff. "Three men are lying dead. Another escaped to a cave."

"And Angel, Sheridan? Is she safe?"

"Aye, Papa. She took the ponies to higher ground." She looked again to her father. "But the tide was coming in quickly and . . . if only I had told Caol the whole story from the beginning, but—"

"Enough, Sheridan, you will hurry and follow the men to your mother. She will require your help, daughter." He shoved the sword into her hands and pushed the skiff back into the water. As he jumped into the boat and grasped the oars, he called to her once more. "Go, daughter."

Sheridan hugged Caol's sword to her breast, rubbing her cheek along the hilt. Last night, she had dreamed that Caol slept beside her. So real, it had been. She lying in his embrace. But when she had awakened this morn, Caol had not been there. Gone. Vanished. When she had spotted Caol atop the cliff, oh, how her heart had soared. She should have known he would wish to search out her story, he being the skeptic.

Keeper of your heart, Sheridan.

Surely, she would be dead now, lying on the beach with the three men, if not for Caol standing in the way of the arrow. "Live Caol, live."

Sheridan strapped Caol's sheathed sword around her torso. She looked back from where they had rowed. The skiff bounced upon the sea as Papa rowed it toward the rock bluff. Oh, how she hoped Papa would find Angel and the ponies safe.

She turned and ran after Vali and the men who were, by now, trudging upward along the pathway to Ferna.

Chapter Eleven

Caol opened his eyes and stared at a pair of brown boots and a woolen skirt that twirled as the woman worked between the fireplace and a table. The embroidered butterflies along the hem danced with the woman's movements.

"How many days have we been wed?"

The woman's skirt spun around and the butterflies traveled in a full circle then fluttered to him as Sheridan approached his cot. She sat upon a wooden stool and leaned down, peering into his face.

"Seven days." Her smile almost appeared, hesitated, then stalled as she scanned his face and touched his head, pushing back his hair.

He grasped her hand and held it to his lips, allowing the simple touch to fill him with comfort. Awake. He was finally awake.

"You will tell Ferna to keep her sleeping potions from me." Vague recollections lingered of him awakening, of him struggling to remain awake, only to have Ferna place a cloth over his face, sending him downward into that bottomless dark pit again. "Sheridan, help me up."

"You will remain in that bed if you wish to tell the tale of these last few days." Ferna's voice floated to him from the other side of the cot.

"A man must tend to his needs, aye?" Caol growled. He was lying on his stomach and attempted to lift his head and turn to Ferna. A streak of pain seared across his back causing him to still. "Then I will piss my bed," he concluded.

A rustling at the foot of his cot caused him to frown and then Sheridan held up a bucket. "Come, I will help you," she encouraged.

"Does a man have no dignity in his sick bed?" Caol muttered, wincing when he shook his head. "Then let us all have a peek at my arse."

"Many arses I have seen in many sick beds." Ferna rattled about behind him and then came into view. "Little do they differ." Her humour wafted toward him and he appreciated her attempt to lift his sullen mood.

Ferna carried her basket of stitching to the door and turned to Caol. "You will remain in that bed, Caol De Ros. Movement will rip the stitches and cause more bleeding." She opened the door and stepped into the twilight, then turned back a final time. "Sheridan, you will use the sleeping cloth if needs be." The wooden latch clattered behind her.

Twas not easy, Sheridan and he working together, to push through his pain, to roll him over and have him relieve himself in the bucket. After, he convinced his wife to allow him to lie on his back and lean against the pillow.

Sheridan worked at the hearth, ladled broth into a bowl and sat again on the stool beside his cot. He made no fuss when she held the bowl to his mouth, indicating that he should drink. When she attempted to wipe his mouth, he grasped her wrist to ensure she held only a napkin rather than one of Ferna's sleeping cloths—a damn piece of fabric dipped in some potion to make one sleep.

"I will not be the one to put you back to sleep, Caol," Sheridan reassured him, almost smiling. "I like you awake." She rose from her stool. "Alive," she whispered as she turned and placed the bowl on the table. She remained standing, arranging and rearranging the few objects on the table as if unsure of what to do next. Or was she simply avoiding the inevitable? Talking with him. Explaining her actions.

"Hmm." His wound ached, nay burned, stirring his sullen mood and coaxing his anger to surface. He had many questions. How had he arrived in their wedding croft? Where was Sheridan's Angel? How serious was his wound? Had the ponies been returned? And why, in hell, had she attempted to return them on her own? With that thought, his anger embraced him fully and he fisted his hands to control it. So many questions. Yet he only had energy to ask his wife a single one.

"Of these seven days, tis the first that I have awakened with you here." He attempted to extend his left arm to point to nothing specific. The pain forced it close to his side. "In our marriage croft."

Sheridan spun around quickly and the butterflies scurried about for a time, disappearing behind the folds of her skirt and then reappearing. That is what his first few days of marriage with Sheridan had been like, a game of hide and seek. She the hider and he the seeker.

"I wonder why you chose to marry." He could not bring himself to include the word *me* in his question. The rejection the word implied, twas like an arrow had pierced him again. Fool, he was. "For you have run from m . . ." The damned word almost smacked him in the face. "For these many days."

"Caol . . ."

Her plea floated to him, attempting to gently caress his heart.

"You must speak, Sheridan!" He lay his hand

on his chest. "Speak to this abandoned husband! Aye?"

Her startled glance equaled his own surprise at his brusque command but he would not soften his stance. Rather than marry him, she could have easily hidden with her Angel but instead, she had accepted his proposal and then—he could hardly bring himself to think it—rejected *him* and *his* protection. He would have her explanation. The truth! He felt that he had been deceived. Damn it all, deceit had landed him almost in his grave. "Speak!"

His sharp demand drew Sheridan's back straighter, her chin higher. She strode to their wedding cot and stopped to stare at him for a time. Then she sat upon the stool. "I will try my best to speak, Caol De Ros. My words do not flow as freely as yours."

"Hmm."

Sheridan lifted a finger to his mouth and shook her head. "Tis time for you to listen. Carefully. Without judgement." Her finger exerted pressure as if she knew he would protest. She studied him and then dropped her hand to her lap, seemingly satisfied. "I married you because, for me, twas a splendid idea."

When he turned his head sharply to glance at her, raising his eyebrows, she leaned in closer. "Twas a word I heard at the dock, bartering."

Caol was sure the golden flecks in her eyes

twinkled brighter. How did she do that? Making her lovely words dance rhythmically off her tongue. Twas not the first time she had caught his attention using this strategy. Clever woman.

"A time ago, a sailor had displayed crimson colour wool for barter. 'Splendid!' he described it. The lovely colour sent my heart beating, for I wanted that wool." Together they looked down at her skirt. Indeed the butterflies were speckled with crimson dots. "For as long as I can remember, tis been the same with you. My heart, you send it beating."

Caol stared at her for a time, wide-eyed with surprise at her clear and honest words. When he attempted to speak, her hand flew to his mouth, covering it.

"Seven days past, never had I dreamed in my life that you would offer to marry me. Twas a splendid idea." The musical lilt in her voice capered about his heart.

When he tried to pull her into his arms, he was certain scalding water poured out of his wound. He drew in his breath, closed his eyes and hissed through his teeth. "I wish you would have shared this with me from day one of our marriage, Sheridan. It would have been splendid."

"Caol De Ros!"

His eyes popped open when she clamped a

hand over his mouth, again.

"You are not to speak. You must listen, husband!" She glared at him, obviously not finished sharing, and he nodded his agreement. She dropped her hand. "Tis not easy, Caol De Ros, to share, for you are often speaking." She nodded her head furiously when he opened his mouth and widened his eyes to feign shock.

"Tis not always easy to share when you . . . you . . ." She tilted her head again, searching for the right word and then spoke softly. "When you speak against our ways." She lay her hand against her breast. "My ways."

When he drew in his breath this time, twas to ward off the pain that pierced his heart. In his humour, in his anger, he had spoken against her ways, her traditions, her parents, her people. All of these had made Sheridan the lovely woman that she was. There were few words to defend his arrogance and to heal the hurt that simmered in her eyes, in her hand fisted against her breast, in her lower lip clenched between her teeth.

He wanted to take her hurt, her pain. And when he drew her into his arms—

"Caol, nay, you are wounded!"

His wound screamed so that he held his breath and lay shaking for a time. But he would not, could not, ever release her. "You are mine. Tis a splendid idea!" he hissed through the pain.

"What did you say?" Sheridan questioned.

"Let us do something splendid," he chuckled, despite the searing pain.

"The sleeping cloth, I am sure you need it." She giggled.

"Hmm," he murmured, and wished that he had the energy to remain awake and talk more with his dear wife, as he drifted off to sleep.

Chapter Twelve

Sheridan opened her eyes and gazed into the darkness of the small croft. She was sure a sound, a slight scraping, had awakened her. Yet, twas only the wind whistling about the hut and the constant boom of the waves against the shore that spoke into the night. And Caol. She smiled and touched her husband's hand. He snored softly beside her in their small bed.

There it was again, a vague scratching. Sheridan pulled herself from the cot and found her way to the table, where she fumbled for the flint to light the tallow. She held the candle high, and turned to each corner in the room, surveying the tiny croft. All was still in the single room. Placing the tallow upon the fireplace mantle, she ran her hands along her arms. The midnight chill touched her bones.

Sheridan tended to the fire, quietly placing a few dry clumps of sod and a handful of coal. The coal was a luxury, really, but Papa had bartered at the dock for a few buckets to keep the fire burning while she and Mama had tended to Caol.

She remained kneeling before the fireplace as she studied Caol in bed. Mama had been amazed that Caol had survived his injury. Carefully extracting the arrow from his body, staunching the bleeding and striving to purify the wound had made it necessary for her mother to pass the sleeping cloth over his face many times. It had been a struggle, for Caol was a fighter in his sick bed, yelling in pain, but swatting away the hands that would help him. She and Papa had held him securely while Mama tended to the wound.

Sheridan smiled at her sleeping husband. Twas the first time she had smiled since his awakening earlier. And twas the first time he had slept on his own, without a sleeping potion, since being brought to the croft.

Yesterday, Mama had supposed Caol was meant to stay in the land of the living a while longer. "There is more work for Caol to do here," she had mused.

Yet Papa had declared, "Tis only Caol's stubbornness that is keeping him alive."

"Could be, could be," Mama had replied with a sidelong glance at Papa. "Takes one to know one, it does."

Sheridan smiled again. Her parents' easy banter had lifted her spirits over these four days when Caol had wavered between life and death.

Sheridan patted her breast, attempting to rub away the memory of Caol lying as if dead on the beach. Day by day, as she had tended him, her hope had grown that her husband would push through this terrible ordeal. Oh, how her spirit had soared when he had awakened earlier this eve.

There it was again. The softest of rattles brought her to her feet to stare at the croft door. The door latch had been pulled through its hole and twould not be so easy for an intruder to enter. She drew a knife from her boot and waited. A scraping sound as if the door was being caressed drew her closer and she placed her ear against it.

"Sheridan?"

She jumped away from the door, a hand resting on her breast, and the knife held high.

"Sheridan?"

Twas Papa whispering from the other side of the door. As she lifted the rope latch, the door opened a smidge and her father squeezed into the room and closed the door. "Extinguish the light, daughter."

"But . . ."

"The tallow," he whispered, placing a finger over

his mouth.

A few strides to the mantel and Sheridan reached for the tallow. She turned to look at her father. He nodded once and Sheridan snuffed the tallow.

The flames at the fireplace had not yet caught on and the shadows crept closer. "Shh," drifted to her as she stood silently in the darkness waiting for . . . she knew not. Twas strange, her father's appearance here, in the middle of the night, standing inside the croft door as if on guard. Trepidation skittered along her back and she took a single step closer to her husband. She was thankful that a second dagger was in her other boot and she grasped the one she held ever tighter, waiting. Could she stand in harm's way for Caol if danger came through her door?

From time to time, the sound of Caol's light breathing and his muttered snore hummed about the room. Sheridan moved her weight to the other foot and rubbed her hands along her arms to ward off the fear that skittered about her.

Twas another slight rattle that brought Sheridan's head up quickly. She peered into the darkness, listening as a small, almost indistinct sound scratched on the floor. She was sure the door had opened and closed.

"Sheridan?" her father breathed. "The light, daughter."

Sheridan slid the knife into her boot and then turned to the mantel to find the flint. Soon the tallow came to life. Tis when she turned back to her father that the flint fell from her hand. Before her stood Justus De Ros and the man called Iain Campbell crowded together at the door. Both men wore heavy dark capes and, in unison, pulled the hoods from their heads. Her father need not have put his finger to his mouth to signal her again, for she stood speechless, so surprised she was, to see Caol's father staring back at her.

"We must speak quietly," Papa whispered. "For Vali the Younger continues to bar all newcomers from the Island. These men have ventured here this dark hour and waited until the clouds drifted o'er the moon to follow the path to us."

In a few strides, Justus de Ros stood before her. He was a smidge taller than Caol but with a similar build. Caol had inherited his father's dark eyes that at times appeared almost black when in the shadows. Each had dark brown hair, although Sheridan spied a few greying strands on the Laird of Rose's head.

"I understand that Alan and Ferna are not the only ones who may call you daughter. Now you are also my daughter." He took her hands and placed something within them. "I and my wife, Lady Brianna, welcome you to our family."

Sheridan looked down at her hands. It was a necklace. One that was familiar to her for Caol had worn it for as long as she could recall. A small wooden heart was threaded through a narrow leather band.

"Caol pulled it from his neck the day Iain Campbell was forced from this Island." Justus De Ros nodded his head toward Campbell and then closed her hands over the necklace. "Campbell brought it straight away to Rose Castle. I knew I must come immediately for it is a signal, a sign that trouble is amongst us." He stepped away from her, looking toward Caol. "Now, since you are the keeper of Caol's heart, will you care for this necklace until he can wear it again?"

Sheridan nodded, unable to find words to speak to this rather formidable man who was now her father-in-law. She gingerly stroked the small wooden heart with a finger. *Keeper of his heart.* These words caressed her own heart and she pulled the necklace tightly to her breast. Caol's wedding night promise echoed back to her, *Forever the keeper of your heart, Sheridan.* What had she promised him?

Nothing!

Rather she had relished in the splendid role of being his wife and being held in his arms. Then she had run from him, and from his promise. Her game of hide and seek had almost cost the keeper of her heart his life. Sheridan slipped the necklace into her pocket, grasping it tightly. She silently vowed that on the first opportunity she would pledge to Caol that she was the keeper of his heart.

Justus De Ros walked to Caol who continued to sleep through this quiet commotion. He looked to Alan and Iain Campbell. "We will wait here for our visitor. It should not be long."

"Papa?"

Papa put a finger to his mouth. "Another visitor, we wait for." His lips tipped in an attempt to smile. "All will be well, daughter."

Sheridan frowned at her father's words, confused. When she would have responded, her father shook his head and touched his lips again.

She knew her father to be a reasonable man, purposeful in his actions and decided to accept his cryptic words for the moment.

Realizing her company was here to stay for a time, Sheridan glanced down at her appearance. Still wearing her day clothes in which she had fallen asleep beside Caol, she righted her headband, pushed her hair behind her shoulders, and patted her skirt. She wrapped her shawl tightly around her shoulders and went to stand beside De Ros.

"After four days, tis the first time he has slept without a potion."

"The wound?" De Ros questioned.

"An arrow pierced his back, below the left shoulder," explained Sheridan. "Mama has done a fine job of removing it and suturing the wound carefully. Caol must remain still for a time to allow the wound to mend." Scanning De Ros' face, she saw the same concern that had embraced her when she had first seen Caol lying on the beach. "He will live," she concluded, and smiled as De Ros released a breath of relief.

"My son is a capable man, Sheridan, able to resolve many issues. Yet, when I heard that Vali the Younger had detained him on this Island, I had to come." A spark of anger traveled across his face and coiled about his words. "I will sit vigil," he stated, walked around the cot and sat upon the stool that was usually Mama's perch. He pulled up his hood and settled back against the croft wall. He looked to the door with narrowed-eyes, "We will wait." Then crossing his arms at his chest, he closed his eyes.

Sheridan gazed at her father-in-law for a time. Even as he feigned sleep, Justus De Ros was an intimidating man. The palpable tension he had brought into her small croft hung heavily in the air. She ran her hands along her arms. The fearful chill still lingered about her. What could he be waiting for at this late hour when the wind whistled at its loudest? She turned to her father. "Papa?"

"We wait, daughter." Then he sat on a chair at the table, crossed his arms upon it and laid his head down. Iain Campbell had already settled upon the dirt floor, his back against the croft door, eyes closed and knees pulled against his chest.

Frustrated, Sheridan determined to be awake when the next *visitor* came to her door on this night. Sheridan reached for the almost empty container of crushed koffie beans that sat on a shelf beside the mantel. She pulled the lid from the container and banged it on the mantel, irked that these men refused to tell her why they were in her croft at this dark hour.

"Shh," drifted to her from her father's corner chair.

She sniffed in response, so be it, and tossed a scoop of the beans into the pot of water that hung at the hearth. When sailors from the big boats had brought a fascinating bean to the dock a few years past, she had bartered for a small container, unable to resist her curiosity. In time, she had learned that these koffie beans kept one awake. For sure, she would be awake and ready for the next intruder to her croft.

Grasping the ladle, she stirred the warming pot of water. It darkened as the crushed beans seeped into the bubbling liquid. Soon a rich aroma wafted about her, calming her spirit as she reached for a cup and poured her drink.

Sheridan settled on the stool beside Caol to knit, to sip her brew and to wait.

Chapter Thirteen

Caol sat straight up in bed, wincing with pain, his eyes opening to a dimly lit croft. A rumble of thunder rattled the shutters.

"Bloody hell, Vali!" Caol bellowed. He would not be fooled this time. Twas no thunder. There was only one person who pounded like the demons.

Wincing again as he moved his head to stare at the croft door, Sheridan and Alan rose from their chairs. Strange that Alan was in this croft in these wee hours of the night.

Stranger yet was to see Iain Campbell standing beside the door, drawing a knife from his boot. When Caol would have bellowed a second time demanding to know what on earth was name was going on, a hand gently rested on his arm and beckoned him to lie back in his cot. Turning toward the touch, he stared into his father's face.

"Da?"

Justus De Ros stared back, touching a finger to his mouth, then signaled Sheridan to sit back down on her stool. He nodded to Alan who stood at the door, readying to pull the rope latch. He narrowed his eyes as Vali the Younger entered the croft in a single stride, glaring at the occupants.

"We have not waited long. Indeed, Vali, you have done well to detect us at this hour." Justus De Ros stated. "Vali the Elder taught you well."

"'Tis a devious occurrence to creep onto this Island in the dead of night." Vali scowled at Justus De Ros. "I have closed the Island to all newcomers until issues have been resolved. But permission to enter would have been granted had you sought it."

"Indeed you are a fool, Vali the Younger," Justus De Ros' words carried an ominous tremor. "Never would I seek your permission or be barred from my own." De Ros rose from the stool. "A bloody fool."

The tension in the room was palpable and Caol knew his father well enough to recognize when retribution was at hand. "Indeed," Caol stated, raising his eyebrows and gazing toward the door. "Fool he was when he barred Iain Campbell from the Island. Look fast, Vali, for there is a knife at your back."

Twas a fine moment to allow Iain Campbell's reckoning for the undeserved beating he had endured at the hands of Vali's men. As Vali turned to face the unknown, he grabbed a wooden chair and swung it high into the air. But Iain Campbell had been set up for the advantage, and rightly so. He stepped aside as the chair crashed against the door. Then he punched Vali in the face, pulled him up from the floor and shoved him against the wall. As Vali struggled against the surprise attack, Iain Campbell held a knife at his face. Vali stilled.

Satisfaction almost warmed Caol but was stalled as he reached out to take Sheridan's hand, preventing her from rushing into the fray. He shook his head feebly, flinching with the pain as Sheridan tugged to be released. Then she relented upon seeing his anguished expression and sat again on her stool.

Justus De Ros walked around the cot and stood beside the two warring men, his attention fully on Vali.

"Tis your good fortune, Vali, that Caol has survived this bizarre ordeal, for the demons themselves would have broken loose had he succumbed to his injuries."

When Vali struggled against Campbell's hold, Justus De Ros shoved a hand against his shoulder, pinning him fully to the wall.

"Rose Castle has always been a friend to this Island." If it had not been the middle of this night, Caol knew his father would have bellowed the words. "We have always come in peace, summer after summer."

He dropped his hands to his sides. "Vali. What bloody notion burrowed into your head that a companion Caol brought to this Island was a threat? That keeping Caol captive on the Island was a good decision?" His father raised his fists a smidge, then settled them at his sides.

"If not for Vali, I might be in the ground beside his father." Caol interjected before his father could continue.

Except for the wind that rattled about the croft, the room was silent. Caol saw his father unclench his fists. His shoulders and back eased from their soldier-like pose.

"Fool," Justus de Ros muttered then nodded to Iain Campbell who stepped away and took up guard-position at the door.

Caol, too, eased himself back against the soft pillow. He had thought that possibly these last moments had been but a dream, yet the pounding ache at his back reminded him that he was definitely awake. He inclined his head to Iain Campbell, a silent salutation of thanks for returning to the Island with his father. Campbell nodded in return.

As Alan righted the thrown chair, Justus shoved Vali toward it. "Speak! What bloody notion compelled you, the new Lord of this Island, to beat up on a stranger who journeyed to your Island in peace?"

Vali stumbled onto the chair. "Grief is a nasty beast. Muddies our minds."

"Hmm," De Ros growled. "You will not cower behind your father's death to rationalize your reckless behaviour." Justus de Ros pulled a chair from the table and sat on it. "Slaughtering ponies, demanding Sheridan marry you, beating Campbell, detaining Caol. Grief, you say? Tis a lame excuse."

Vali rubbed his hands over his face. "Blinds us. Makes us fools for a time."

"Tis shite you spew, Vali," countered Justus De Ros.

Vali righted himself on the chair. "You are aware that Vali the Elder rests on the northern point of the Island?"

"Aye. Campbell told me as much." Caol noticed how his father stared at Vali, long and hard. Even Alan chose to quietly sit down at the table in the roaring silence.

"Tis a strange place to have your father buried. Setting the body afire and blazing it to sea is your tradition." De Ros frowned. "Vali the Elder held fast to tradition. Another foolish decision, Vali?"

Sheridan pushed Caol's hand aside and rose. "Before he died, Vali the Elder insisted he be buried at the northern point. In this way, he believed he could still watch over Angel."

Startled, Caol lifted his head a smidge, looking at his wife, surprised that she spoke of Angel. Sheridan had been so insistent that the woman's existence remain a secret. He had planned to tell his father about the woman when he returned to Rose Castle, yet if his wife wished to speak of her now, twas good. Best to get the topic out into the open. Caol rested his head against his pillow, his energy waning and his wound demanding stillness.

"Daughter." Alan spoke for the first time since Vali's entry, his pallor flushed. "To reveal Angel's existence, we risk her safety."

"Angel?" Caol's father leaned back in his chair and looked from Alan to Sheridan.

"Nay, Papa." Sheridan strode to the table where the three men now sat. "To be sure, Caol will share Angel's story with De Ros. Tis the proper thing, to speak of her now."

"Angel?" De Ros questioned again. "How did this conversation change from Vali the fool, to an Angel?" His father turned to Caol. "You will explain, Caol. Now!"

"But the words must be spoken away from this Island, daughter, so no one else hears," demanded Alan, sitting higher in his chair.

"All are asleep at this hour, Papa. And who will hear, but us, for the shutters are pulled and the door is closed?" Sheridan looked around. "Soon I will be gone from the Island with Caol. Angel will lose my presence, my friendship. We must speak of a plan for her, now, in the dark of night when no one listens." She glanced at Vali. "Then all can be put to rest."

De Ros slammed his hand down on the table. "Enough! I have journeyed here to ensure my son's well-being. But instead you speak of an Angel?"

Caol admired his wife's courage, as she glared at Alan, refusing to retreat. Twas just that, her quiet courage that had drawn his attention over the years.

"Da. Angel, she is a woman who was washed ashore on this Island some twenty years past," Caol stated. "She is the mystical Angel of the Island."

"Angel of the Island. Twenty years?" echoed De Ros.

"Tis not your place to speak of these things, Caol," Alan hissed, standing abruptly and glaring at Caol. "You know not of what you do, the risk you bring, when you speak these words aloud."

Caol bit the inside of his mouth to prevent himself from speaking rudely to Sheridan's father. So weary he was from fighting against his pain and, now, against Alan's anger. Twas not like Alan to be in such an agitated state. Yet a plan must be put in place to reassure Sheridan that her Angel would do well after her departure. Mayhap he spoke for his own selfish purpose. But bloody hell, he would not be stalled from getting off this Island with his wife.

Caol carefully turned his head, looking again at his father. "All these years, Angel has been hidden in a cave on the north point of the Island, to ensure her safety." He was sure his father-in-law might have throttled him had Justus de Ros not raised his hand to halt Alan's advance. Even Sheridan placed a hand on her father's shoulder.

Alan cursed and backed away, dropping his hands to his sides.

"I would hear more of this tale of a woman cast to this shore all these years ago. Hidden," whispered Justus De Ros.

Alan slumped into his chair and clasping his hands, he slid them across the table, leaning low over them. "I have given my oath, my pledge, to Vali the Elder that Angel's tale would ne'er pass my lips in all of my days."

"Another story, I know, from twenty years past," began Justus de Ros. "Of a babe, a foundling, without name or history, discovered at an old woman's door. Hidden to ensure her safety." His father leaned in closer to the others at the table and lowered his voice. "I have raised the babe as a daughter, known as Bonnie of Rose."

"All these years, you had allowed us to believe

that Bonnie was the child of your wife, Lady Brianna."
Alan's tone was accusatory.

"All these years I, too, have given an oath, my pledge of silence, to keep my foster daughter safe, her story a secret. We only shared her story with few and allowed many to believe what they willed," breathed Justus De Ros. "Like this woman, Angel, the old woman declared that Bonnie too must be hidden to ensure her safety. I seek any information that might help my foster daughter discover her true beginnings."

"I will speak of this story, for I have given no oath," Vali stated.

How could Vali possibly speak about the Angel's story, Caol wondered. Sheridan had said that only she, her parents and the Elder had known of Angel's existence.

"Nay!" Alan pushed to his feet and stood glaring at Vali.

"I knew naught of the woman until my father lay on his deathbed." Vali spoke low. "There, he attempted to tell me Angel's story. Too weak, he was, to tell me the full tale. But bits and pieces, I have, of the woman, and of Sheridan," Vali concluded.

"Of me?" Sheridan stepped away from the table and sat again on the stool, her eyes were large and flashed with unspoken questions. "Papa?"

Alan slammed his fist on the table, then stood,

shoving the chair out of his way and walked to the fireplace, staring at the flames. "The Elder was addled when he spoke these bits and pieces to you, Vali."

"Nay. I say he was not," countered Vali. "For his eyes were clear a final time, for a moment, and his words audible." Vali's whispers floated about the room. "Earnest, he was, and he gave to me the responsibility of Angel's protection in his final moments. In his weakness, he was unable to tell of her location. He spoke of Sheridan's association with her. When Sheridan hid the two living ponies, I hoped she could lead me to Angel's location." Vali looked at Sheridan and Alan, then at Justus de Ros. "But they have refused to trust me and will not share Angel's hiding place."

Caol eyed Sheridan who looked at Alan, confused. Silent. She had not told him this part. That Vali the Younger also sought Angel's location and not just the ponies. The pain throbbed at his back. Indeed. The events of the last sennight were_leaving him exhausted and confused, even disappointed. Would Sheridan ever trust him enough to share her life fully with him? "Hmm."

Sheridan turned to Caol, shaking her head. "I did not know this part, Caol. That Vali wished to know Angel's location. That he wished to protect her. He had only demanded the location of the ponies." She turned back to the table. "Papa, you did not tell me this part."

"You must stop this blather, Vali! At once," Alan demanded. "For it helps no one. You would do well to measure the risk of speaking these words, man! Sheridan will be gone from the Island within days. Tis good that she will live at Rose Castle." He turned again to stare into the fire. "None will be the wiser."

"The wiser of what, Papa?" whispered Sheridan.

"You will speak, Alan. The truth! You must!" Vali hissed. "If not but to purge the Island of lies that you have held so close all these years, and that bring danger to this place. Enemies may still linger here."

"I would know this tale, Alan," urged Justus De Ros. "For I sense my foster daughter's plight may well be connected to this woman called Angel. I would meet her, Sheridan." Justus De Ros stood. "Take me to her whilst the night is still dark."

"Nay," Sheridan stated and walked to stand between the table and the door. "For a nighttime visit will frighten Angel. I will go to her when light arrives and ready her. Then, we can all journey there and speak with her."

Alan pounded his fist upon the fireplace mantel, then knelt and threw a handful of coals and a few clumps of sod onto the fire. The flames jumped higher, then simmered low again as Alan rose, turning to Sheridan.

"Tis your tale, too, daughter." He sighed deeply, resigned. "I know your mother will want to share in its telling."

"My tale, Papa?" echoed Sheridan.

"Tis the tale of how your mother and I were given responsibility for you, for your protection, my dear daughter," whispered Alan.

"Papa," breathed Sheridan. "You speak in riddles."

For a time, Alan stared at her, then shook his head. "No longer will I, daughter." He stepped toward the door. "I will fetch your mother."

A rattle at the door, and a whispered, "Tis I", caused Sheridan to hurry to open it. "Mama?"

Iain Campbell stepped aside as Ferna entered the croft.

"She comes. She comes," the older woman murmured. "The Angel of the Island arrives." The wind whipped into the house, swinging the door wide. The moon had found its way from behind the clouds and its light spilled into the small croft, as all watched for the one Ferna had so fervently announced.

Caol raised himself higher on his cot to see. The woman walked majestically along the path that led to the croft. On this eve, Angel wore a robe of white and appeared the mystical character that was told to the children of this Island. Twas quite spectacular how the moonlight glowed around Angel, emphasizing the paleness of her skin, and shimmered about her long white hair. She surely was a fanciful fairy tale, a ghostly figure dressed in white, sparkling in the moonlight. Almost celestial, Caol thought, and pinched himself once to ensure that he was certainly not dreaming and he was still in the land of the living. He was.

As Angel stepped into the croft, Vali rose and Ferna clasped her hands to her breast. Indeed, his father and Iain Campbell both took a step back. Caol was sure he heard Justus De Ros whisper, "Jesu" as he made the sign of the cross.

Angel stood just inside the door, grasping a bundle to her breast. Her eyes sought Sheridan.

"Welcome, dear friend," Sheridan whispered. "You are a long way from home, this eve."

"Who is this woman?" Caol's father had recovered from his surprise and his commanding voice pierced through the whispers and secrets of this night. "What in God's name is going on?"

"This is Angel, the Angel of our Island," Sheridan stated.

The gentle warmth in her voice danced about the croft and stroked Caol's heart.

Chapter Fourteen

"Angel?" Justus de Ros murmured. "Angel of the Island?"

Sheridan moved closer to Angel, her heartbeat quickening, as she watched her father-in-law roll the words around on his tongue. His gaze hardened as he eyed the woman.

"I would know this story of Angel!" he demanded, taking a step closer to the woman. "I had come to resolve a ludicrous tale of my son held captive. And now I stand before another strange tale." His gaze fell on each person in the small croft and then returned to Angel. "You will speak. Indeed! All of you will speak, and tell your part in these strange happenings!"

"Tis true, Da, tis a peculiar story," Caol struggled to rise higher in his bed. "But the woman does not speak. . . "

"She cannot speak," Sheridan intervened as she

moved between Angel and De Ros. "And neither does she usually venture atop the Island to be with people." Sheridan clasped her hands at her waist for Justus de Ros' steely stare was intimidating. She slid her gaze to Caol. Twas a challenge to explain a secret that had been tucked away for many years. When Caol nodded his head and smiled at her, she found the courage to continue. "Let us speak quietly, to keep this tale amongst us, to ensure Angel's safety. And—"

Sheridan turned quickly as Angel stepped closer to Caol and pulled from her bundle a carefully folded cloth. Again, her husband struggled to sit upright in his bed and Sheridan hurried over to help him position himself.

Angel shook the cloth into the air and it floated down to cover Caol's already blanketed body. Twas Caol's plaid, the De Ros weave of blues and greens. The wrap that Caol had left Sheridan sleeping under when he had ventured up the stone steps.

As Sheridan tucked the wrap around her husband, Angel pulled another folded cloth from the bundle. What was Angel up to? Sheridan watched carefully as Angel shook the cloth and gingerly laid it atop Caol's wrap. "Angel!" whispered Sheridan in surprise. Twas a blanket, displaying intricately embroidered pictures. A masterpiece. For sure, twas Angel's handiwork.

The blanket covered the length of Caol's cot. Twas a large piece of cloth that had tinges of water marks upon it. Surely it was a piece of material ripped from the sail of a ship. Possibly a piece of debris from a shipwreck that, at times, was found along the shore. To be sure, Vali the Elder had likely brought this discovery to Angel, for he had known how much she enjoyed stitching pictures.

Sheridan leaned over the blanket, studying it, amazed at Angel's skill. The colourful scenes upon the cloth were delicately stitched, of people and ships, ponies and cliffs, seasons and weather, crofts and food, the sun and moon and various stars. And the grandeur of the sea, its waves billowing high, spilled across the pictures, embracing each scene. Oh, how this masterpiece was elegantly woven, each detail precisely stitched creating a whole picture. Sheridan placed her hand against her breast. Tears pooled in her eyes for joy or grief, she knew not which. But, to be sure, the scenes upon the blanket told a story, of love, of loss. Twas life!

Sheridan caressed a corner of Angel's wonderful tapestry with her hand. Even the edges of the cloth had been carefully hemmed, tacked beautifully with stitching of crimson wool.

"Angel," Sheridan breathed. "Tis lovely. Lovely."

"Sheridan." Caol touched her hand. "Look,

here." He pointed to a scene in a lower corner of the needle point. Twas a small picture, almost hidden, of a girl looking up as if studying this tapestry and the story it told.

Sheridan gasped, for it was she, or at least they were her eyes, the darkest of brown with golden flecks. And there was her nose, a straight nose, with that sprinkling of freckles. She scrunched her own nose for a moment, then rubbed it. When younger, oh, how she had hoped she would outgrow those freckles.

The face in the picture was wreathed in embroidered wisps of brown wool with curls, stitched about in a whimsical style, much like her hair. Angel had even lightly accented some of the tips with yellow wool to indicate the bleaching rays of the sun.

Sheridan took a step closer to Angel's handiwork, leaning over it in search of other pictures of herself. She cautiously touched the young child staring into a pony's face and gently caressed the young woman sitting along the cliff edge staring out to sea. She giggled when she recognized herself standing at the dock, hands akimbo, bartering with a sailor. And there she was, standing with Angel, at the Elder's cairn. She shook her head in amazement as she recognized even more events as she grew up.

"Angel," Sheridan breathed, "You have not ever shown this to me. Tis so beautiful. And a fine blanket for Caol as he recovers."

Angel gazed at Sheridan for a moment, a quiet smile edging her mouth. Then the woman carefully untied two small ribbands attached to an edge of the tapestry. Angel's hands fell away and she looked to Alan and Ferna. Then she took a few steps away from the cot to stand in the shadows.

Twas strange, that glance between Angel and her parents. Why had Angel ventured here, to this croft, in the silence of night? She never came atop the cliff except to walk amongst the ponies at night. A chill skittered along Sheridan's spine and the back of her neck tingled. Something was out of sorts.

"What is it Angel? Papa? Mama?" Sheridan questioned. "Angel, you have not journeyed to my croft to bring blankets to Caol!" When Caol gently grasped her hand and pulled her toward him, she slumped upon her stool and stared at Angel and her parents. "What are you about, Angel?" she whispered.

"We will sit," Alan directed. "To hear a tale long kept silent." He looked at Justus De Ros. "And also bizarre. Mayhap unbelievable."

Her father-in-law leaned against the croft wall, arms folded across his chest, waiting, as Alan brought two chairs to set beside Caol's cot. Vali dragged a chair to place at the foot of the cot and sat upon it. Iain Campbell remained standing at the door.

"Tis a story that is true, we vowed would ne'er cross our lips," Sheridan's father began, leaning into the small group that huddled around the bed. "Vali's insistence, here this night, to tell the story and Angel's arrival has convinced me . . . we must share the story now." Her father turned to her mother and stared at her for a time. Then she nodded her head.

"Papa, I do not understand. What story?"

"Silence, daughter." His voice was soothing and coaxed Sheridan to listen, much like the tone he had used when she had been a young child. "For I will only speak the story this one time." He grasped Ferna's hand. "Then ne'er will we speak it again." He pulled Ferna's hand close to his heart and then gently placed it again on her lap. "Twenty years past, a daughter lived. Two summers, she was. Full of life . . . and health." His smile was fleeting.

"Me, Papa?"

"No, daughter. Another child, she was. She cheered our hearts for too short a time."

Tears glistened in her father's eyes and her mother dabbed at hers with a handkerchief.

"In her third spring, our daughter grew ill. Twas a wicked season, full of storms and chill. Snow fell, rare though it is on the Island. Twas accompanied by a vicious wind and a sickness crept into our daughter's chest." Her father patted his own. "As the snow faded away so did our wee lass." Her father's gaze fell upon Sheridan. "She died."

Twas a jarring tale. Bizarre and a wee bit scary. A chill crept into Sheridan, making her pull her shawl closer.

"Her shell remained in her small cot, but her spirit . . ." Alan breathed deeply, looking to Ferna as she placed her handkerchief in his hand. "Her spirit had passed on, gone to her creator." He sniffed loudly and wiped the handkerchief under his nose."

"Papa? Mama?" Sheridan whispered. "Of whom do you speak?"

"We speak of daughters, my dear," her father replied. "Of one taken. Of one given."

"Given?"

"Twas a strange night that our wee lass was taken. I stepped out into the darkness to seek help, to bring the women to help Ferna prepare our child's body. The wind, oh, how it howled through the bushes, laughing around the corners, mocking me in my grief. I was sure the demons themselves had been unleashed to torment me."

Throughout this strange tale, Caol had gently caressed his thumb across Sheridan's hand in a soothing rhythmic pattern. She focused on the motion, striving to calm her rising emotions. Who was this dead child? Why had this story not been told to her?

Why did her father's gaze, tormented and misty-eyed, display sorrow and joy in equal measure?

"That eve, I came upon Vali the Elder on the trail leading to the dock. He had just come from the north point of the Island. The wind had been blowing ever so wild that the fire he would light to guide the ships at sea had refused to burn." Alan stopped and looked at Ferna and then at Sheridan. "He was not alone on that trail."

"Who Papa? Who was with him?"

Her father bent over the tapestry, pulling the ribbands that Angel had untied earlier. A small flap of material lifted up.

Leaning closer to see what was beneath the fold, Sheridan saw a beautifully fashioned ship, embroidered delicately amongst blue and grey waves.

"You, my daughter."

Nay, it could not be. Surely, she had not heard her father's hushed tones correctly. "I am hearing nonsense, Papa," Sheridan stated. "You will speak it again, that part."

"I speak the story clearly, for it is ever engraved upon my heart," her father continued. "Angel walked with Vali, carrying you—a small child, appearing quite dead." He raised his brows and placed a finger to his lips when Sheridan would have protested. "Yes, daughter, twas you. A ship had smashed against the northern point of the Island, unable to conquer the winds and the waves of our North Sea. You had washed ashore. As had Angel. Vali the Elder pulled you from the waters and knew he must get you to Ferna if you were to survive. Twas then I told him about our dear dead daughter. When he entered our croft and saw one child dead and the child he carried alive, he shared with us a most peculiar tale."

Sheridan's peace and calm had long fluttered away. Gone, vanished. The knot in her stomach was slowly rising, reaching for her throat, readying to choke her. Snatching her hand from Caol, she jumped up from her small stool. Never had she liked ghost stories and for sure, twas what her father was now telling. Buried ghosts!

Sheridan hurried to the table, pulling the flint from her pocket, to light another candle. The tallow that lit the small croft had burned low and the shadows were creeping close around her. She did not understand this story. A story of a wee lass that, she believed, was she, but wasn't. She yearned to run from the croft, from the bizarre story her Papa was telling. Twas too confusing, too strange and—

"Sheridan."

Caol's voice caressed her heart. He was calling to her, beckoning her to return to him. She closed her eyes for a moment and breathed deeply, then turned back to the group, to Caol. She set the tallow on the side table next to her husband's cot and sat again on the stool.

Caol smiled at her for a moment, recapturing her hand, scanning her face, her hair. His slow and steady caress on her hand resumed and she was sure he whispered, "Splendid." The silent breath of that dear word wafted about her heart, tenderly calming her.

Caol turned to Alan. "What was this most curious tale that Vali the Elder shared with you?"

"Angel and the child she cradled in her arms were not the only survivors from that treacherous wreck. Indeed. The child's mother and an older sister also endured the damning seas and were resting in a cave, while the Elder sought help for the injured girl."

Mother! Sister!

Sheridan's heart slammed into her ribs with the sudden realization that this man sitting across from her, the man named Alan, was not her father. Her eyes darted to the woman named Ferna! Twas the first time in the telling of this tale, in her whole life, that these two people she called Papa and Mama . . . simply were not!

"The mother, who was heavy with child, had implored Vali to tell no one. She, her children and her maid, who was Angel, they were fleeing from danger, their lives in peril. She spoke briefly about a murderous villain who lived along the northern shores of Norway. Surely, if they were found, they all would perish. She would only release her daughter to Vali if the maid stayed close to her."

Alan's gaze fell on each person in this huddled group and then he settled his eyes on Sheridan. "A plot formed that eve. I speak of a gift taken and a gift given. A daughter for a daughter. To bury one daughter and resurrect another. For that is what was done. Vali the Elder vowed he would care for our little daughter, secreting her shell to an unknown spot. And the other child? Ferna applied her healing magic, bringing her to good health. You awakened, Sheridan, days later, of a pleasant disposition, and too young to understand your perilous journey. Both daughters were similar in age and appearance, as bairns go. The winter had been long. Our daughter had been sick and unseen for weeks. When you, our second daughter, ventured forth from our croft and into our community, all appeared well. Indeed, Sheridan, all rejoiced that you had made it through these perilous months, none the wiser about the covert happenings of that treacherous night."

"My name, Papa," Sheridan demanded. "What was my name?"

"Vali the Elder refused to share details of your

mother and sister's identity. He found voyage for them from the Island. Angel remained, her appearance too noticeable, recognizable, for her to venture forth with them. The Elder built her a home in the cave and allowed her to watch you from afar," explained Alan. "Twas I that gave the woman her name, Angel, for her appearance speaks of brightness and light. Surely sent from heaven above. And you, dear daughter, when you stepped out of our croft in the warm spring breeze, we had given you a neke-name, Sheridan. For we explained to all, that you had recovered from a daunting sickness and had brought brightness to us during a very dark time."

Sheridan snatched her hand from Caol's. Her head pounded, the room swirled with all staring at her. Even Angel's gaze seemed less friendly, more foreign. She did not recognize any of these people!

Her eyes snapped to Caol. Her husband? If she were not rightly Sheridan, then surely he could not rightly be her husband. She stomped her foot on the ground as she rose from her stool, pounding out that dear word she shared only with this man—*splendid.* She looked to the croft door. She did not belong here anymore.

A sudden movement in the croft shadows brought her attention back to the huddled group. Angel! The woman walked to the small table beside

Caol's cot and lifted the burning tallow high above the tapestry.

Sheridan caught her breath, surprised, for the tapestry had come to life! It was blazing with golden sparkles that danced and shimmered across the scenes. Surely, a masterpiece, it was. For those golden sparkles breathed life into each scene, accentuating the colours, the seasons, the story that was told—her story.

Alan and Ferna moved closer. Even Justus De Ros lowered his arms and stepped into the huddled group.

"I did not know of this!" Alan caressed the tapestry and rested his hand on the fabulously embroidered boat. He looked at Angel. "Tis gold. Specks of gold, stitched into the tapestry, ever so carefully, hidden."

Vali the Younger rose from his chair. He ran his hand over the tapestry, smiling as he touched pieces of gold. Twas a certain gleam in his eye that caused Sheridan to move away from the group and toward the croft door.

When she would have reached for her cloak, Angel took her hand pulling her closer again. Closer to the lie. Twas all a lie. Each picture embroidered upon that tapestry and each piece of gold hidden was a lie! An untruth.

She was not Sheridan. Twas not her story. She shook away Angel's hand and swiped at the tapestry, mussing it. When Caol tried to take her hand, she stepped away.

Sheridan looked at the croft door. She would run from this place, from this Island, and go to her real people. The mother and sister that her Papa—nay Alan—had described.

Grabbing her cloak, she turned to the door. Iain Campbell stepped away from it as she rushed forward and pulled it open even as voices called her back.

"Daughter!"

"Sheridan!"

But she was none of these.

Everything! A falsehood!

Chapter Fifteen

Sheridan sat on the edge of the cliff, her knees pulled to her chest, staring out at the grey ocean. At her back stood bits and pieces of the old abandoned soddie. The roof had collapsed ages ago. Now only two walls stood, one with a dilapidated door still hanging from leather hinges. The other walls had crumbled to the ground, creating large moss-covered mounds about her. She felt much like this old soddie—broken! The story of her lost lineage had cut to her core. To be sure, a piece of her soul had been severed from her, leaving a deep and aching wound.

Never in her deepest thoughts, when a child, or now a woman, had she ever imagined that she belonged to another. That she was a daughter to another. She leaned her forehead against her knees. So confused she was, but she pressed down on the churning myriad of emotions readying to boil over and sweep her away.

Who was this woman, her mother, who had found voyage on a ship and then refuge here on Vali Island? Surely it had been happenstance to have landed on this small rock. A plot of land on the northern sea, isolated, if not for the boats that docked here from time to time.

What had the woman been running from? Papa—nay, Alan—had said the woman then had fled from this Island. Could she not have waited until her young daughter had recovered? Yet that woman, her mother, had left her. Nay, she hadn't left her, her mother had . . . Sheridan breathed deeply and then mumbled that word that had been roiling inside her . . . "*Abandoned* her." There, she had said it.

She felt no better.

Sheridan shook her head in protest. The dreary ocean seemed to smash more loudly against the rocky shore as if agreeing with her. Her mother had chosen to flee without her. She blew a puff of breath, anger surging against this unknown woman.

Sheridan growled in frustration, rubbing her temples and winced. Sheridan of Vali Island was no better than that woman from long ago. She was just like her mother, for she had fled too. So jolted she had been, she had run from the croft, from the truth that Pa . . . Alan . . . had whispered. And she had run to this lonely forsaken spot. She stretched her neck, back and forth. Last night, she had hunkered down, hiding behind the old soddie door. When she had finally fallen asleep, she dreamed of voices calling her name and hands snatching at her. Upon awakening this morn, her body ached from lying on the hard, cold ground with no pillow or cushion. Twas as if she had fought a long and brutal battle.

Sheridan looked about at the remains of the old soddie, attempting to distract herself from the confusing thoughts that niggled about in her head. She had played here as a child, sometimes with friends and even with Caol. Nay, she would not think about him for he was no longer hers. She fisted her hands to capture the thread of grief that wafted about her. She would use this time in hiding to make a plan. She would find her people. Her real people.

Sheridan refused to turn when a rustle from behind indicated someone had entered this spot through the dilapidated door. A deep sigh ending on a gentle sniff identified the intruder.

"We have looked long and hard for you," her mother—nay, Ferna—stated. "And you have been here all along."

Sheridan closed her eyes for a moment and hugged her knees closer. She clasped her hands tightly to prevent the well of emotions from flooding over. A flutter of air and a brush of an arm against her own told her that Ferna sat beside her.

"Sheridan."

The word wove its way around her, tightly embracing her, drawing her into its rhythmic beat. "Our brightness," Alan had often declared when she had been young, a twinkle touching the corners of his eyes, the words dancing across his lips.

Nay! She would not succumb to that warm memory, to those days of joy when she belonged here with these people. These dear, dear people.

"I am not Sheridan."

Three kittiwakes squawked overhead. Were they agreeing with her, or reprimanding her? Another flew into the mix, joining the birds in their chorus, in their joyful revelry. Oh, how she envied that bird, for it knew its place, its role, gliding on the wind, searching for its food, joining its flock. What would happen to the bird if suddenly its identity were ripped from it? Would its singing end? Would it thrive alone? Would it still be a kittiwake?

She felt stripped of all she had known. Even her name held no meaning. Worthless, it was.

"You are Sheridan and so much more," Ferna countered.

"A lie, I am. My life has been a lie."

"Nay," Ferna whispered.

"And yours also!"

Sheridan turned quickly as Ferna gasped and flinched as if scalded by hot water. Oh, how she had promised herself she would not look at Ferna, would not yield to her loving gaze. But twas no loving gaze Sheridan saw in Ferna's face but one of anguish, pain.

Sheridan sat straighter, nose a bit higher. She would not give in to the guilt that pushed against her for accusing Ferna of lies. Yet she still bit down on her tongue to stop her words, her accusations. Oh, how she did not want to care about this woman, did not want to love her.

"Nay, daughter," Ferna fisted her hand at her breast. "My life has been real, lived in truth, for I have felt the pain of it." A sniff, a swipe at her eyes. "And the joy of it."

A silent moan bellowed from Sheridan's heart. Ferna's words wafted about her, caressing that place of memories, of relationship she had built with this woman, this dear woman. Nay! She would not falter on Ferna's anguished words. "A mother speaks truth!" she seethed.

"A mother protects," Ferna stated.

"A mother does not abandon her child." Sheridan hiccupped on a sob, then drew in her breath, choosing to hold tight to her anger rather than succumb to her grief. She glared at the grey waters below. The tide was creeping closer, the waters rising higher, crashing about the jagged rocks that stood as sentinels in the shallows. On that long ago night, she wondered, had the ship capsized at sea or smashed against the Island's rocky shore? Sheridan frowned, bitter, remembering the first time she had met Angel. The woman had been overjoyed to meet her. Meet her! She shook her head. Naïve, she had been.

"Vali the Elder and Angel. All! All of you!" Sheridan glared at Ferna who narrowed her eyes and stared right back. "You led me to believe that it had been only Angel washed ashore!"

Ferna nodded her head, then shook it, blowing out her breath. "Twas a surprise, on that long ago day. You surely loved to follow the ponies and that day you had followed them all the way to the north point. Surprised, Vali the Elder was as he had just come up the hidden steps and walked out from the gorse bushes. And there you were, staring back at him," Ferna reminisced. "You, being so curious, had to look behind the gorse bushes and had to follow the steps downward to the sea. Twas never intended for you to find Angel, to meet her . . . again." She raised her hands and then resettled them in her lap. "The Elder could not persuade you to stop, to return to the top of the cliff." Ferna shook her head again. "What could the Elder say? He knew, and so did Angel, that the secret had to be kept to ensure safety for you . . . and for

Angel."

Sheridan bit her bottom lip, preventing a smile. She remembered the day she had found Angel. Vali the Elder had beckoned her to stop and when she did not, had followed along behind her. He had always been so kind to her. But now she'd rather stew in her anger. Twas safer, than allowing that wall of emotions to come tumbling down upon her.

"All of these years, I kept Angel a secret. I could also have kept the whole story, my part of the story a secret." Sheridan crossed her arms. "Truth!" she fumed.

The older woman shrugged. "Twas happenstance that you found Angel." She fell silent. Then she drew her familiar deep breath and sniffed. "All!" Ferna emphasized the word. "All of us did this to help you, to protect you." Ferna slumped her shoulders and rested her chin in her hand. "Tis hard to know what more to say to you, Sheridan. I must trust that the decisions we all made were to protect you . . . and Angel. Your mother would not release you to us until we had all vowed that the tale of that strange night, twenty years past, would ne'er pass our lips."

"You have met my Mother?" Sheridan leaned closer to Ferna, scanning her face for this truth, then quickly turned away. She would not love this woman who looked back at her.

"Nay, only Vali the Elder saw her, communicated with her. The woman refused to be seen or to even give her name, so convinced was she that death awaited her and her children if found." Ferna narrowed her eyes as she finished. "Those hunting her had to believe that everyone had drowned at sea."

"I died that long ago night." The sorrowful truth coiled around Sheridan, taking her breath. Cold watery arms seemed to slither around her, pulling her down into that ocean, embracing her like a burial shroud. She only snapped her eyes open, shivering, when Ferna caressed her softly along her cheek.

The older woman lifted Sheridan's fisted hand, holding it close to her heart, and stared out to the sea. "Only one daughter died that night, the one that grew from my womb. Perhaps I abandoned her, for she ne'er received a proper burial." A raw tenderness quivered along Ferna's words. "The other daughter lives, the one that grew from my heart." Ferna's gaze returned to Sheridan and she squeezed her hand quickly. "She is treasured. She is Sheridan." Ferna rose and stepped toward the door, readying to leave.

"Do you think of her?" The question spewed from Sheridan before she could catch it and stuff it back down into her angry thoughts.

For a time, Ferna was silent. Her skirts billowed about, snapping in the wind. Then a deep sigh ended on a gentle sniff. "A mother ne'er forgets."

The old door creaked behind her.

Chapter Sixteen

Hands. Dead hands. Bony fingers clawed and grasped for him as he fell into the black pit. He bellowed as a hand latched onto his arm. His eyes flew open.

Caol peered into his father's face.

"High time you awoke," his father stated, studying him. "Tis good to see you rested. Improved." A smile hinted about his father's grim expression. "Thank God, you are well."

Caol gazed about the croft, remembering, relieved the pit he had tumbled into was only a dream. "You will keep Ferna from me." He hissed the words through his teeth. "Tis damn irritating, it is, to have my wife run from the croft and a sleeping cloth flung over my face."

A chair scraped on the dry dirt floor of the croft as Alan rose from it and came to sit upon the stool that was always saved for Sheridan.

"Ferna has brought you back to life and would not see your wound ripped open again. In your attempt to follow Sheridan, the wound bled." Alan offered Caol a cup filled with Sheridan's brewed koffie. "Drink. Will warm you some."

Caol accepted the drink and was pleased to note that only a little pain emanated from his wound as he moved his body. "How long have I slept?"

"Ferna insisted that you sleep for another day," his father replied. "The wound has benefitted from your rest." Weariness was etched about his father's eyes and at the corners of his mouth. "Ferna had us stand guard over you while she is out and about."

"I would speak to Sheridan." Caol noted that the croft door was closed and the shutters pulled. Where was his wife? "You would bring her to me, Da." The glance between the two men caused Caol's ire to rise. "I will not be held prisoner by Ferna. I will have my wife beside me."

His father took a deep breath and looked briefly at Alan before he shifted his glance to Caol. "Sheridan refuses to return to your croft."

"I will go to her then." Caol scanned the room and spied his tunic hanging on a wooden peg next to the bed. He flung the covers aside and reached for the tunic, snagging its end. The wound pinched below the shoulder and he breathed deeply to stay the pain.

"Sheridan wishes all of us to let her be." A tremor of worry wended through Alan's words.

"I will not." Caol flicked the tunic over his head and shoved his right arm through its sleeve. At least neither man was attempting to stop him. Twas only the pain below his left shoulder that prevented him from shoving his left arm into the tunic. Bloody hell, he must be dressed and out of here before Ferna returned. He noted that the bedside table was free of sleeping cloths. "I would need help, Da."

"Not I, son," his father replied, crossing his arms at his chest. "I will not face Ferna's wrath."

When Caol looked to Alan, the older man shook his head. "Ferna and Angel followed Sheridan. Never could they leave their lass to handle such a battle alone. They will coax her back."

"Battle?" Caol questioned, shoving his left arm through the sleeve with such force that his whole body shook against the pain of it. He flung his legs over the side of the cot and sat for a moment, measuring the ache as it slowly subsided.

"Anger," said his father. "'Tis part of grief."

That lonely word—grief—so quietly spoken, floated about the room and then softly landed upon Caol's heart. It spurred him on and he looked accusingly at Alan. "Why did you wait all these years before you told Sheridan this strange and bizarre story. Tis a shock learning about it as a woman."

Alan lifted his head, narrowing his eyes. "Caol, I stand on my decision to remain silent . . . and know we made the proper choice to protect Sheridan." He raised his shoulders then shook his head. "Twas not an easy decision, nor even an easy way to live."

Caol frowned and looked to the door. Dear God, his wife had run from this place last eve, spooked. There was no clear answer to such a situation.

He returned his gaze to Alan. "Mayhap, if you had even told me where I might find Sheridan, the morn I came to your croft. Surely much of this turmoil could have been avoided."

"Sheridan assured us, the afternoon you were wed, that she would share Angel's story with you. We trust our lass. She is a woman. Capable. Twas not our place to interfere." Alan crossed his arms and studied Caol for a moment, then lifted his brow. "Mayhap, Sheridan delayed in telling you because she sensed you were not willing to hear her story, her words." He folded his hands on his lap. "Her ways."

"Hmm," Caol breathed. Indeed Alan knew how to twist knives with his words. Irritating. Yet, truth be, if he thought back to the day he and Sheridan made love at the water hole, he realized now, she had been readying to share this story. But what had he done? He had spoken first, expressing his disappointment in learning about the ponies from Vali the Younger, and Sheridan had remained silent. If only he had kept his mouth shut and listened to her. Twas true, sometimes it was hard for Sheridan to speak when he was doing all the talking.

"Neither must I justify my decisions or actions to you, Caol," Alan continued. "But this much will I say and then no more. On that long ago night, the woman, Sheridan's mother, had spoken so urgently to the Elder, begging him to reveal naught of Sheridan's story. Certain, she was, that if a tale of a woman and daughters ever circulated and they were found, they would be killed. Best to let all believe they had drowned at sea. She, her two young daughters and the babe she carried within her."

Alan lifted his hands into the air and then dropped them again to his lap. "The maid, Angel, is noticeable, her colouring. She had to be hidden for her own safety and Sheridan's safety." Alan rose and poured himself a cup of brew and then turned again to the men. "Nay Caol, twas not a decision made lightly. Changed the path of all our lives. For even my first daughter did not receive a proper burial." He sniffed and rubbed his hand below his nose. "Tis not a day goes by, I do not think of that wee bairn."

Alan sat again on the stool, shoulders slumped as if the burdensome story weighed too heavily. Then he straightened his back. "If only the Elder had not shared the story, bits and pieces, with Vali the Younger. Surely all would be well on this Island. Yet, the son would be the new Lord of the Island and the Elder, in his attempts to pass on the responsibility, shared the story. Too weak he was, to tell it whole and reveal Angel's location." Alan took a sip of his koffie. "The Younger in his new role, attempting to learn of Angel's and the ponies' location, did not handle the situation well." He shook his head. "He might have given Sheridan extra time to save more of the ponies. Many believe he should have. He did not. Fool, he is. Some people on the Island want our Council to vote on whether the Younger should continue as Lord. Tis challenging to follow a tyrant and indeed Vali the Younger has become one. Tis difficult to know what the answer is to all this. But when Sheridan chose to wed you rather than Vali, I suspect it did not bode well with him. You became a captive, Campbell was beaten." Alan downed the contents in the mug and set it on the side table. "Ferna and I, we saw your marriage as a blessing. Now Sheridan would easily leave the Island with you and move away from any danger. With no one the wiser as to her beginnings. Her secret never to be revealed. Her safety ensured."

"Blessing?" A smile tilted the corners of Caol's mouth. "We have your blessing then, Alan? For you had not given it to us on our wedding day."

"Aye. The blessing given at the hearth and marriage bed, Caol? A door slammed in my face, man, preventing the blessing from being given!" Rising, Alan picked up the mug and poured himself another cup. He turned to Caol. "This is now my blessing, Caol. Prove yourself worthy of Sheridan's choice!"

Those words again! Twas the second time in these few days that Alan had questioned his merit as Sheridan's husband. Caol rubbed the back of his neck. His new relationship with his father-in-law was, indeed, precarious. Dear God, he had taken an arrow for Sheridan. Was that not enough for Alan to see him as worthy? He shook his head. What did it matter? He would take a hundred arrows for her, no matter how Alan measured his worth.

His father laid a hand on his shoulder, a life-long gesture to calm, to reassure. Caol determined to change the subject. To take the conversation away from Alan's bruising words and scowling face.

Caol looked over his shoulder at his father who sat on the other side of the cot. "And Bonnie, Da? Could it be possible that she is the unborn child this woman carried? The time line is exact for both Bonnie and Sheridan. Twenty years ago, Bonnie was left at an old woman's door and Sheridan was washed ashore."

"Indeed. Tis too coincidental, I think, that

Sheridan and Bonnie share a similar story," Justus De Ros concluded. "Sheridan, a two-year-old bairn, was brought to Ferna. Bonnie, a new-born babe, brought to an old woman's door. If Bonnie is that unborn child, it would appear the mother made it to the mainland of Scotland." His father scratched his head. "Although, the two young women's appearances are verra different. Bonnie is tall. Sheridan is petite. So I must wonder. Yet both have golden specks in their eyes and freckles sprinkled across their noses."

Caol smiled at his father's words. He imagined Sheridan's lovely face. "Ah, five freckles across Sheridan's nose and six painted under each eye." He felt his body stir, his heartbeat quicken, desire nudged deep and low. He rubbed a hand across the back of his neck. When he found his wife, he was going to . . . Twas the silence that made him lift his head and see the two older men studying him—Alan frowning, his father smiling. A warm blush crept onto Caol's face. Indeed! He needed a distraction. "Bonnie knew of her plight from an early age. Twas part of her legacy." Caol looked at Alan who glared back.

"We shared Bonnie's whole story with only a few," Justus De Ros explained. "All believed that Bonnie came to Rose Castle with Lady Brianna. Few knew she was found at the old woman's croft. Bonnie came to Rose Castle wrapped in her seal skin blanket.

Brianna's Silkie, she was named. Twas only this spring when she had to flee from danger, that Bonnie's story was shared with more people, the guards and families at Rose Keep. Never did we share it beyond the lands of Rose." He paused. "To keep her safe. Away from danger, aye?"

Caol supposed his father was correct. But still. Bonnie had always known herself to be a foster daughter. When danger had confronted her, she was not surprised that she had to flee.

"Danger," Caol mumbled. "Alan you spoke about danger, here still on this Island, last eve at the telling. I saw Vali strike down three of the men. Indeed, he must have wounded the fourth as well."

"Tis hard to know if the fourth man was wounded," Alan explained. "He escaped to a cave along the shore. When I ventured to the shore, I did not see him. Vali the Younger also searched and claims he could not find him. Does the rebel remain on the Island, or did he escape?"

"And Sheridan, then? If the villain is still on the Island, she is not safe!" Dear God, he had missed a lot in these four—or was it five—days he had lain in this cot. He looked quickly at the door. He could not be here when Ferna returned.

He rose from the bed and stood for a time allowing his sense of balance to return. A few steps brought him to the hearth where his boots stood. He smiled. Sheridan had been busy for his boots had been wiped clean and the water marks had all but disappeared. He eyed his father, who just raised his eyebrows at him. He knew he would receive no help from Alan. Pulling a chair, he sat upon it and tugged on his boots, swallowing often as he warded off the sharp ache at his back. He took the knives from the stone hearth and shoved them into each of his boots.

"Iain Campbell stands guard at the old soddie," explained Alan. "An eye on her at all times, even if she does not know it."

Caol turned in the chair sharply and tried to conceal the wince that jarred him. He would not get through that door, if either man knew his wound had been compromised. He was sure the bandage was damp. He strode to the cot and snatched his plaid and wrapped it around his torso, over his shoulder and tucked it securely at his waist.

"She refuses to return to us," Alan explained. "Ferna is visiting with her now at the old soddie, below the Elder's resting place."

The pain that twisted Caol's heart had nothing to do with his wound. Twas sheer sorrow for his wife who seemed to be lost. While he had slept for another day, Sheridan had sat at the edge of a cliff surrounded by the remains of a dilapidated soddie. That hovel was naught but an old heap of sod without a roof or place for a hearth and bed. "Grief," mumbled Caol.

"Aye, grief," Justus De Ros echoed, nodding his head.

"Grief, tis a battle that leaves one cold and empty," concluded Alan.

Caol nodded at the men. Twas a lonely word. *Grief.* That old soddie, a cold and empty piece of dirt, sat at the edge of a cliff and had provided no comfort to his dear wife. He had to get to her.

Caol lifted his sword and strapped its belt across his chest. The weapon at his back exerted pressure against his wound. Perfect. Would stay the bleeding. "Da? How did I get through the grief of losing my mother and my sister?" If he knew how he had risen from that dark place, he might be able to help Sheridan.

A shadow of pain skittered across his father's face and then he smiled at Caol. "Lady Brianna. When I married her three years after your mother's death, she became your mother. She slowly drew you out of your sullen state and made you pleasant again."

"Da!" Caol protested. Yet he had to agree. He had been an angry child after his mother's death. Poorly behaved, nasty at times. Angry at everyone, including his father. He had to give his father credit for keeping him close. Another might have sent him away to a monastery to learn his lessons or to a family member in another clan. "I thank you, Da, for hanging in there with me."

Caol walked to the door, pulled on his cape. Twas Alan's voice, gentler now, that made him turn again to the two men.

"Caol, grief is a nasty beast. But once it is tamed, then life and love can again thrive. You must be prepared, Caol," Alan stated. "For our Sheridan is in a very unpleasant state of mind."

Caol inhaled deeply and tugged on his hat to just above his eyes.

"You best be on your way before Ferna returns," his father cautioned. "You passed her test."

"Test?"

"Aye." His father continued. "Only if you could dress yourself were you allowed to leave the croft."

"Ferna said that we were also to check your wound prior to your departure. Any seepage would indicate you must remain in bed," Alan told him.

Ferna! He had to get out of here or she'd be checking his wound and see the tell-tale sign. Caol backed toward the door. He had to get to Sheridan. He fumbled for the latch and opened the door. "You tell Ferna that—"

"Tell Ferna what?"

Caol swung around too fast and gripped the

door frame, holding himself still, while the pain seared through his left shoulder.

"Tell you that I am well," Caol sputtered to his mother-in-law and then hurried past his jailer.

He stomped down the pathway, his steps in rhythm with that dear name he held in his heart—*Sheridan, Sheridan, Sheridan.*

Chapter Seventeen

Caol strode along the path that he had walked with Vali just a few days past. The old soddie sat close to the Elder's burial spot and just behind the water hole that Sheridan and he had swum in the day after they had wed.

As he approached the top of the path, he turned east toward the ocean and jogged along a trail that led over a rocky plateau. Just as he stepped onto the dirt pathway, the metallic clash of a sword pulled from its scabbard resounded beside him. He turned quickly to see a man stepping out of the shrubbery brandishing his sword high. Caol grasped the handle of his sword and pulled it from the scabbard mounted on his back.

Twas when the man stepped onto the sun-filled pathway, that Caol lowered his weapon, relieved. "Put that bloody thing away," Caol growled, "Tis I." Only when Campbell lowered his sword, did Caol shove his into the scabbard.

"The sun's rays blinded me and I could not recognize who strode the pathway," Campbell explained, looking slightly embarrassed.

Indeed, the late afternoon sun was glaring down upon the path. Caol glanced beyond Campbell to the clearing where the old tumbled-down croft sat. The sun rays shone brightly about the remains of the old structure. He hoped that Sheridan's welcome would be as warm. His skepticism told him otherwise. "How goes it?"

"Only Ferna has passed along this trail," Campbell explained. "Last eve, I followed Sheridan from the croft. When the moon took refuge behind the clouds, I lost sight of her along the main pathway." He looked toward the croft and then back to Caol. "Twas a challenge to find this hidden trail."

Twas true. The trail had not been trod for years. Brush had grown over the footpath and the entry to the trail was obscured by overgrown gorse bushes. Sheridan was clever and had chosen her hiding spot well.

"I thank you for standing guard. And for delivering my necklace to Rose Keep." Thank God Campbell had chosen to do so, for he had known his father would see it immediately as a call for help. He rubbed his hand where the necklace should have been hanging. He would have to remind Da to return it to him as he likely had tucked it away at Rose Keep.

"Tis my small part. Aye? To keep watch as you unravel this mystery." It had only been in these recent months that Rose Keep had ventured to interact with Iain Campbell and his people. But Campbell was proving himself trustworthy, one who could be relied upon.

Campbell inclined his head toward the old croft. "The woman, Ferna, appeared unhappy when she left the soddie." He waved his hand toward it. "You best go."

Caol wended his way along the dirt path and came to a few rock steps. Descending, he finally stepped onto a lower plateau of grassy land where the dilapidated croft stood. Or had stood. For only two walls remained, standing as sentinels, and revealing naught of what was behind them. He walked to the far right, around the walls and stopped.

Wrapped in a dark cloak, hood pulled tightly, his wife sat along the cliff edge as still as . . . death. His stomach roiled with that thought and he took a step closer, for rarely had he witnessed his wife so— he squeezed his eyes shut then opened them again— so dark and lifeless. The woman he knew was usually in motion, working with the ponies, knitting, bartering at the dock or preparing meals at the hearth. Indeed brightness described her. Suddenly images of

Sheridan descending the cliff wall and running from the croft marred his pleasant thoughts and he rubbed his hands over his face, striving to bring his attention back to this dreary place. He was relieved when she raised her hand to push the hood higher on her forehead. Twas a slight movement but it indicated that she lived.

Caol strode forward and stepped over a mound that had once been a wall of this croft. He stood beside Sheridan. Twas when she flicked her hood from her head, appearing startled to see him, his shock slammed into his belly and weakened his legs. He lowered himself to sit beside her.

Caol could not help but stare at his wife for she had visibly transformed. The Sheridan he loved had disappeared. He understood now why the cape appeared so dark for each of the delicate and brightly embroidered decorations had been ripped from it. Her skirt no longer had crimson butterflies fluttering along its hem. Only shadows of tiny holes made by an embroidery needle remained. The headband that often held her hair away from her face had been torn in two and each piece tethered a braid on either side of her head. Her lovely brown curls lay tightly hidden in each thick plait. When he reached for her hand to feel her warmth, she quickly tucked it beneath that dark and dreary cape.

"Hmm". The oath he had given to her on their wedding night wafted about him: *I will stand with you, fight for you, protect you, Sheridan, until our days are no more.* So the fight had begun.

"I would hold your hand Sheridan," Caol soothed. "Tis comfort for both of us." In the few times that they had made love and held each other, neither could resist the other's touch and caresses. If he could just touch her, mayhap the healing would begin.

Caol's hopes heightened as Sheridan withdrew her tightly clasped hands from underneath the cloak. Slowly her hands opened, revealing the little pieces of woolen threads she had pulled from her clothes. To his surprise, she flung her arms high and threw the colourful threads over the cliff. The bits hovered above them for a time, the colours melding into a bright display. Then a gentle wind captured them, scattering the pieces back around the two of them. The fragments fell over them, on them, settling on their hair, on their shoulders, on the toes of their boots and dotting their clothing.

When Sheridan attempted to brush them off, he grabbed her hand. "Nay, I like having you on me, over me—and under me," he crooned.

She slid her eyes to him. A blush rising on her face satisfied him that possibly he was breaking through her glum exterior.

A crimson thread, precariously balancing on the tip of her eyebrow, tumbled onto her eyelashes. He snatched her other hand to his chest as she tried to flick it away. When she blinked, it fell onto her lip and then settled on the hem of her cloak.

"Tis hard to make one so *splendid* disappear," he said. He tugged each strip of the hairband free from its braid, smiling as the tresses loosened and the curls tumbled out, framing her face. When she attempted to push him away, he held her hands again, a wee bit more tightly. Finally she stilled, but turned her face away to look out to the sea.

"When I was in school, first at Edinburgh and then Paris, I met many lovely young women—talked with them, danced with them." He smiled inwardly when she turned again to him, eyes narrowed, as if she was not completely happy with his schoolboy antics. "All the young women dressed in their finery, braids and ribbons, silks and lace. Verra lovely." He added those two final words for emphasis. Dear God, he was fighting for her, for them, and he wanted her to enter this battle too. To fight for their union. Was it possible to break through this steely wall that Sheridan had built around herself? He thought he heard her sniff and he was sure she lifted her chin a wee bit higher.

"Yet in my mind's eye, I kept imagining delicate butterflies stitched to a lace collar or a row of pink flowers embroidered about a wrist band." One time, he had even found himself counting freckles on the face of a lovely woman and felt disappointed when she was one freckle short of Sheridan's count.

"You, Sheridan of Vali Island, kept calling me back, again and again, summer after summer." When he pulled her onto his lap, she did not protest but neither did she relax against him. "Sheridan, you are splendid." Slowly, she turned her face to his as though not believing his proclamation. "When you agreed to marry me a sennight past, I was thrilled." He chuckled. "And scared too. I have longed to share all my thoughts and feelings I have had for you over these years. But for now, for this time, I will say, Sheridan, you are mine, dear wife, held so tenderly in my heart. And I am yours. Throwing snippets of thread over the cliff will not change this, Sheridan."

"Sheridan does not exist. She is a lie!"

When she abruptly rose and strode away from him, he followed. Standing beside her, he studied his wife as she drew the cape tightly about her and stared out to sea. A somber sense of satisfaction grew within him to see her anger erupt—that steel wall was beginning to crumble. Yet her sorrow, her grief, was palpable and it coiled tightly about him. Picking a yellow thread from her shoulder, he twirled it across his fingers and then slid it across his lips. "Sheridan of Vali Island exists as surely as this yellow thread does." He released the snippet to the wind but it quickly fluttered back and landed on her hand.

Sheridan swiped it away. "Nay! A made-up life."

A thread of fear twisted about Caol. Such a declaration threatened her existence and those who loved her dearly. He took a step to stand in front of Sheridan and looked into her eyes. The golden specks that had danced there for as long as he could remember had dimmed below her furrowed brow. "But how? How has it been made-up? Have you not lived your life fully, Sheridan of Vali Island, feeling each part, believing in each moment? Never did you speak or walk falsely. Twas a true life."

She shook her head and waved her hands as if to dismiss these ideas. "I am not Sheridan of Vali Island. I am not your wife!"

Twas like an arrow piercing him again, to hear those words pass her lips. Caol placed his hands on his belt and widened his stance. He could not lose her. He would not!

"When we stood before the priest and you stated your marriage vows to me, did you pretend while you spoke, Sheridan? Was your commitment made-up? And when we make love and you whisper my name, tis like a tonic that is poured over me. Tell me, now, is that sweet whisper false, or do you feel it, live it, as deeply as I?" Again she stepped away and again he followed to stand before her, forcing her to look at him. He would not surrender this battle. *I will fight for you, Sheridan.*

"Sheridan of Vali Island, you named our union *splendid*. That dear word danced across your lips and twirled into my heart, locked there forever. Tell me now. Did you speak a falsehood, pretend it to be, or did you speak true?"

Sheridan turned her head from him, clenching her lower lip in her teeth and placed her fisted knuckles against her mouth.

She was a formidable opponent, this wife of his. Caol lifted his hand and tenderly caressed Sheridan's face along her brow, brushing away a tear that spilled down her cheek. There was only one strategy left, in this battle. Was he brave enough to use it, to say it? Caol calmed his breathing, and allowed his pulse to slow, its pounding subsiding in his ears. Twas a sacred moment. God in heaven, help him. "Sheridan of Vali Island, I love you."

She turned quickly to him. "Caol."

Her breathless plea floated about him. Dear God, he loved hearing his name tremble from her lips. A sweet surrender he held dear during these early married days. Might it be a sign that possibly the battle could be won?

"Caol, how can you proclaim your love for me? A woman who is called Sheridan, but is surely another?"

When he took her hand, she stepped closer to him. His hope soared for her, for him, for them. "You dear woman, you have danced amongst us, capturing our hearts." He placed her hand on his chest. "My heart. Sheridan of Vali Island."

The golden flecks in her eyes brightened as she slid her hand along his chest to his heart. "Twas all true," Sheridan whispered. "When I stood with you before the priest. When I lay in your arms, each utterance, each caress is felt deeply." She slid her arms about his neck and he held her close. "I love you Caol."

Her words, soft and melodic, wrapped gently about his heart, his soul. Indeed a balm, calming his doubts.

Sheridan snuggled closer to him as he tightened his embrace. For a long time, they stood silently, holding each other, while the wind gently danced about them and birds sang overhead. Twas special, holding Sheridan, her heart beating rhythmically against his own. She nestled her face against his neck and when he felt her tears, he caressed her back slowly.

"Twas a shock, Caol. To learn of my lost

heritage." She fisted her hands at his shoulders, hiccupping on a sob, then lifted her face to his. "She left me. Never to return."

"Grief." He gently held her away from him. "Leaves a hole in our hearts."

She shook her head. "I do not know if my heart will mend."

Caol recalled his own grief for his mother all those years ago. He had filled that hollow place with anger and ugliness. In time, love had driven the bitterness out. He hoped his love for Sheridan also might help mend her broken heart.

"How can I grieve for one I do not remember? And yet I do." She quickly rubbed a hand across her wet eyes. "A woman who chose to leave me?"

He, too, had angrily grappled with the same question. How could his mother have left him? How could she have died, despite his angry objections?

Caol leaned in closer to her. "Do you wonder, Sheridan? Was it a choice?" He had never expressed this thought aloud and rubbed his chest, frowning. For indeed, in this moment, he was sure the faint heaviness that had sat on his heart for all these years, that sorrow for a lost mother and sister, had suddenly lifted, diminished, gone. When he looked over the cliff, glancing out to sea, he felt his fear of heights drift away on the wind.

"Hmm," Sheridan breathed. Her eyes were narrowed and she shook her head.

Caol raised his brows, surprised at her use of his favoured response. So his wife was not ready to accept the idea that mayhap her mother's presumed choice to leave her had been no choice at all.

Healing would not happen overnight. He would spend the rest of his days loving away her pain. He looked forward to it. "I reassure you, Sheridan, we will search for your lost heritage. Mayhap we have already found a piece, for we wonder if my sister, Bonnie, may be the babe your mother carried."

She only stared back at him. "Caol."

Dear God, the way she spoke his name, twas like a tonic, a potion, she sprinkled over him, holding him captive. He took a step closer. "I give you my word. Your lost heritage is a treasure to find."

Sheridan nodded and leaned into him. Twas a pleasure to hold her, to comfort her and feel that a smidge of her pain had diminished. He was sure her face appeared less scrunched with angst, her brows rising a wee bit higher, her lips softening a tad.

"Sheridan?" He kissed each of her hands tenderly, smiling. "Your parents wait for you at our croft. Anxiously. I think we should return together and speak with them to alleviate some of their worry." When Caol reached for her elbow to escort her from this forlorn spot, she stepped away to stand at the cliff. She shoved her hands into the pockets of her skirt and scanned the shore below.

"I am worried for Angel," Sheridan turned back to Caol, frowning. "I have not heard her sing since last eve. I will return to speak with Mama and Papa. But for now, I must visit with Angel, to reassure her that all will be well."

"Tis not safe for you to venture to Angel," Caol insisted. "Come, we will go together." When he extended his hand to her, Sheridan looked down, focusing on what she pulled from her pocket.

"My necklace?" Surprised, Caol accepted the trinket that Sheridan handed to him. "How did my necklace find its way into your pocket? For I sent it with Iain Campbell hoping he would take it to my father."

As he caressed the small wooden heart, Sheridan reached out and gingerly touched it with her finger. Caol locked his finger with hers and then lifted it to his lips.

Chapter Eighteen

Sheridan smiled into Caol's dark eyes as he lightly kissed her finger. Twas amazing, it was, that a single caress from him could soothe her heart, comfort her thoughts. She was not the same person she had been last night when she had ventured to this forsaken spot. His words, his caresses, his declaration of love, had renewed her, given her hope that together they could find her lost heritage.

Sheridan stepped closer to Caol. She could not *not* love him. Whoever she was, her heart called out to him, this splendid man that stood before her. She rose on her tip-toes to tie the necklace around his neck. She must visit Angel and reassure her, but . . .

Sheridan could no longer resist pulling Caol close, kissing him, dancing with his tongue, tugging off his hat, pulling away the leather band from his dark hair and lavishing in the caresses of it as it poured over her hands. Oh, how she wanted Caol to pour himself over her, taking her warmth, her body and she loving him. As Sheridan pulled at his belt that held his sword, loosening it, Caol flinched.

"Your wound, Caol. We will stop. Now."

But as she lowered her hands to her sides, Caol's arms came around her shoulders, her lower back, pressing her firmly against him, sending hot desire burning through her, enticing her arms around his neck.

Her lips sought his, caressing them over his seeking mouth and down along his neck. She spiralled in the pleasure of discovering his rapid pulse just below his earlobe. When she slithered down his body, there was such joy in his chuckle, in her giggle, as he tumbled down with her. Her hands stroked under his tunic, lifting the material away, pushing his plaid from his shoulders, running her hands across his chest, down along his arms, savouring the pressure of his body on her.

All at once, Sheridan snapped her eyes open and looked at the sky. Someone had walked into their space.

"Caol, we will stop."

"Hmm. I think not Sheridan." He suckled her bottom lip, then flittered his mouth along her neck, lowering his lips to her collar bone where he had untied her cape and blouse. "Tis well worth the minor pain at my back."

Twas not easy to resist Caol's touch but Sheridan forced herself to take hold of his hand beneath her skirt where it was massaging, stroking high on her thigh. "Tis Angel, Caol. She is here."

"God Almighty." Caol pulled his hand away and collapsed upon her, shielding her from Angel's eyes, swooshing desire from her, and probably from himself. "Tis not good, Sheridan. Strange Island. Too many gazing upon my arse." He lifted himself enough to place his hands on either side of her. Was there a small glimmer, a twinkle in his eyes? He shook his head. "My arse is for your eyes only, wife. You will pull my tunic down."

Once Caol was fully covered, he rose from his spot, even tugging her skirt down from around her thighs, and strode to the far side of the soddie. He looked out to the ocean while Sheridan positioned her clothes rightly. When she scanned the area, she saw Angel standing around the corner of a wall, her back to them. For sure, Angel had not intended to intrude.

Sheridan spied Caol's necklace on the ground, swiping it up as she rose. She followed Caol and stood in front of him, reflecting the humour that sat in his eyes. She appreciated Caol's sense of humour—most times.

"Tis a strange Island, wife," Caol caressed her

cheek. "We will finish later in some other strange place, I think." He winked through his smile and then kissed her.

"You speak nonsense, husband. For this Island is a beautiful place." She smiled when he grinned. "For it was in this place that I learned to love." Sheridan lifted Caol's necklace as he continued to stare into her face adoringly. A flash of desire sparked through her and she quickly tied the necklace around his neck, securely this time.

"Your father gave it to me when he arrived last eve." She stroked the heart.

"Tis your heart, Sheridan. My oath to you." He tugged the leather strip from around his neck. "Tis a Rose tradition, to give the heart to those we treasure. My father gave Lady Brianna a wooden heart years ago. He fashioned one for each of his children, instructing us to pass it on to the one who claims our heart." He held it out to her. "Will you let me be the keeper of your heart?"

"Caol," she whispered, fingering the wooden heart again, eyes fluttering up to meet his sober gaze.

"You are beautiful, wife," he whispered, smiling, as he tied it at her neck. "Indeed. Splendidly beautiful."

His words filled her with joy, with warmth, shoving away the angst that had filled her, that had almost choked the love from her. The love she felt for Caol, for her parents, for this Island. For Angel.

Sheridan turned quickly. The woman still stood with her back to them. "I will visit with Angel, Caol," Sheridan turned to her friend. "I must speak with her. Reassure her."

Caol tugged at her hand. "Please, Sheridan, invite her to join us at the croft."

"Caol. Tis a risk for her to venture atop the cliff in these daylight hours."

Sheridan turned again to Angel. The woman stood looking at them, holding a basket of wool in one hand and her flute in the other. "She will be seen if she comes to our croft. I will visit with her here." Sheridan stepped toward her friend. "You go, Caol, to the croft. I will meet you there."

"I cannot leave you here alone. An eye on you at all times, Sheridan." Caol rubbed his hands over his face. "What if harm comes to you? I cannot bear the thought." He stopped, hesitated, then continued. "Angel must be invited into our realm and live amongst us. Solve problems with us." Caol snatched his hat from the ground, smacking it against his leg. "Hmm. You cannot keep running to Angel, hiding when there is a problem!"

At another time, the disappointment etched

across Caol's face would have made her stomach quiver, cause her throat to seize. But not anymore. Sheridan drew in her breath and then released it. Twas the first time she realized that Caol's disappointment was bound up in fear, his fear for her safety. Possibly even his fear for the survival of their relationship. Reassurance was the remedy, not running to hide. Sheridan stepped closer and placed her hand gently on Caol's. "I will not hide again." She lifted his hand to her heart. "Ever. You have my word, my love."

The angst sketched across Caol's face melted into a smile as he enfolded her in his arms. Twas wonderful to have him hold her and to believe her promise, her words.

Caol spoke against her ear. "It is believed a few of the men who caused trouble on the Island may still bring harm to you. I will be down the path." He kissed the top of her head, then turned, nodding to Angel and walked around the old walls, out of sight.

Angel approached Sheridan, smiling hesitantly.

"Dear friend," Sheridan said. "We have much to talk about while we mend my clothes."

A smile spread across Angel's face as she sat down upon a mound of sod and pulled two needles and a ball of crimson wool from the basket. Sheridan joined her and the two women began to stitch butterflies and flowers.

Sheridan opened her eyes to the pre-dawn grey. She was sure that someone had stirred the firepit. When she raised her head to peer through the misty dawn, a hand slammed over her mouth. She attempted to rise, to push the hand from her. She bit it and someone cursed. She stilled when a dagger flashed in front of her face, squinting to see through the white mist that hugged the land.

"You listen well!"

Sheridan threw her head to the side when the tip of the dagger touched the end of her nose. The hand fell away. A stale breath of alcohol wafted about, telling her the assailant's face was just behind the dagger.

"You will be coming with us." He grabbed her arm and pulled her to her feet.

"Vali!" Twas all she could do is whisper his name. The shock of recognizing him, the Lord of this Island, knocked the breath from her.

"We have waited a time for you. If you come along without a fuss, your white woman lives," he snarled and shoved her around so that she faced

Angel.

"Angel!" Sheridan breathed. Surprised she was, to see a man standing beside her friend, holding Angel's arm behind her back and covering her mouth with his other hand. Twas the same man who had run into the cave, the day on the beach. "Vali, what are you about?"

When Sheridan reached for her Angel, the assailant flashed a knife in front of the woman's face. "Nay," Sheridan moaned. "Vali, you told us you did not find the fourth man when you ventured back to the cave."

Vali grabbed Sheridan. "You will listen well, lassie."

His spittle peppered her face. The man was drunk! Sheridan turned her head and looked toward the dilapidated walls of the old soddie. How had they ventured past Caol? He and Campbell had stood guard over the pathway to this soddie throughout the night. Had they wounded Caol? Should she scream?

Vali yanked her arm so that she looked at him again. "Don't even think it. You utter one word for help and this time an arrow goes clear through your Caol."

"Nay, Vali! Drunk, you are." She attempted to pull her arm from his grasp. Her heart pounded too fast. "You do not know what you are doing. This man who guards Angel is one of the rebels."

Sheridan looked again toward the place up the trail where Caol had stood guard, but the walls of the soddie blocked her view. The shadows shifted as a streak of morning light grew across the horizon. A meagre ray of sunlight shone against the soddie walls. The light calmed her spirit, gave her hope. She would scream and—

Sheridan swung her head around when Angel whimpered. Against the paleness of Angel's face, a trickle of blood appeared on her cheek.

"Ang—" A hand clapped over Sheridan's mouth and she stared into Vali's reddened, blood-shot eyes. If she could just reach the knives in her boots.

"Tis only the beginning, Sheridan, of what will happen to the white woman," Vali growled, his eyes flicking toward Angel. "You will listen well to what I have to say or those you love will not live to tell of this tale."

A surge of anger rose high in her breast. The scoundrel! Twas true what Papa had said. Vali had become a tyrant. The ponies had been returned to pasture and Vali had appeared satisfied. What more did he want?

As Vali lowered his hand from her mouth, Sheridan looked again to Angel. Oh, how she loved the woman dearly and did not wish her to come to harm. Angel was like a . . . a mother to her. Strange that she would recognize this fact at this moment. Her real mother had fled, yet had left her with two mothers in her stead—Ferna and Angel. She slid her gaze to Vali. "What have you to say?"

"We will be taking a boat ride. Leaving this Island, we are. A ship awaits us at sea." Vali pointed toward the edge of the cliff. "Come. We will follow the old pathway to the beach."

Deceiver! Vali and his accomplice had obviously climbed the trail from the beach to this small stretch of plateau. That pathway hadn't been used in years, eroded by the elements and destroyed by fallen stones. Now she understood how they had sneaked past Caol. Vali had not passed Caol at all.

"Coward!" Sheridan murmured, pulling her arm from Vali. "You are a drunken coward. I challenge you to call for Caol, to see how far you will get."

Angel whimpered again and Sheridan gazed at her friend. The rebel held his knife to Angel's face.

Vali's whispered hiss floated to her. "Your choice, lassie. Who do you choose? Your white woman can live and travel with us or she dies and we can summon Caol."

There was no choice in this. She could not bear to see Angel wounded and neither could she bear to leave Caol. She thought again of her knives tucked into each boot. If she screamed for Caol and pulled a knife, could she pull it fast enough? Her gut told her if she tried, they might all die.

Her hand instinctively touched the wooden heart on her necklace. Once she and Angel were off the Island, Caol would never learn where they had gone. Would he wonder if she had run off again, run and hidden away? She wrapped a fist around the necklace. Caol's necklace! The small wooden heart that hung from it was surely a treasure. For a moment her spirit soared.

Sheridan slid her gaze to the basket that had held the wool. It sat by the cold firepit now, empty but for the gloves that she had put there last eve. She could deceive too!

She rubbed her hands together and looked desperately at Vali. "Please Vali, my gloves. May I take them with me?"

He gazed at her for a moment, narrow-eyed, then nodded. Surely he could not read her mind.

Sheridan knelt at the basket, her back to Vali. As she lifted her gloves, she tugged the necklace from her neck and dropped it into the basket.

They ventured down the rugged trail in single file, Vali leading, and the man who had dared to harm Angel trailing at the end. The stones and dirt were loose and several times, she and Angel grabbed onto a branch of a low bush to steady themselves. The tide was slowly creeping higher and they waded through the shallows to where a skiff rocked upon the waves.

Vali's accomplice drew a short piece of rope from his boot. "Your hands," he growled, staring at Angel and reaching for her hands.

"Nay, Vali. You will not tie her." When Sheridan shoved herself between Angel and the accomplice, Vali twisted her arm high on her back. She held her breath to stay the pain.

"Shut your mouth, Sheridan. Your Angel's life depends on it." When Sheridan remained silent, Vali tilted her arm a smidge higher.

Sheridan eyed the rope and then looked to Angel. The blood on her face had dried. Twas only a surface wound this time, but what next? Sheridan nodded in submission and Vali released her. Rubbing her arm, she cringed as she watched the man pull Angel's arms behind her. The woman gasped in pain as the rope was given a final tug.

When Sheridan attempted to follow Angel into the skiff, Vali stepped in her way. "You will each board a separate skiff and be guarded well on our journey to the ship."

Panic rose. "Nay. I will stay with Angel." She lunged at Vali but only stumbled backward, almost losing her footing. She squeezed her eyes closed to stay the tears. She had to keep her head.

The rebel had climbed into the boat where Angel was already sitting. Vali shoved it into deeper waters and then dragged Sheridan onto dry ground.

"Your white woman can live. The man rowing the boat will not harm your white woman as long as you follow me to the skiff over yonder." Vali turned and pointed to a small boat a distance down the shore, moored in an inlet. It floated in a tide pool and had almost risen above the crests of the rocks that surrounded it.

Twas time to run, to scream, to pull her knives from her boots . . . she caught Vali's eye. He watched her closely, measuring her thoughts. The sneer on his face, the evil in his eyes convinced her that Angel would die if she attempted to escape. Sheridan looked back to gaze up at the cliff top. *Caol come, come, Caol.*

Her only hope did not appear.

Vali grabbed her hand and pulled her along the shore to the skiff. She had to stall him, stop his treacherous attempt to take her from this place. Caol might still see her.

Sheridan pretended to stumble along the shore, feigning exhaustion from the trek down the cliff trail. "We will go slower, Vali. Please." She stopped abruptly and pulled her hand from Vali's grip.

"If I have to carry you to that skiff and dump you in it, I will." Grabbing her arm, he pulled her along the shore again. "Walk, dammit."

"You will tell me Vali, why you do this." She pulled her arm free, glaring at Vali. When he pulled his knife from his waist, she determined to walk beside him slowly.

"I will have your treasure, Sheridan." He shoved her higher along the shore away from the rising waters to where small rivulets ran in erratic patterns along the sand.

"Treasure?" She grabbed his arm. "Vali, take Angel's blanket and the gold hidden there. It means naught to me. Please Vali. Call Angel back. I will tell no one of this."

Vali threw her hands off and she stumbled backward, splashed through a rivulet and landed on her bottom. "Nay, Sheridan. Much have I learned these past days for there is a reward for you, your sisters and your *real* mother," he snarled. "Even for Angel. I need not your blanket. Caol can claim it." When he loomed over her, she scuttled back a smidge. "In memory of you, for he will never see you again."

Sheridan's anger pushed her to her feet. "You saved Caol. You helped get him to Ferna. You make no sense." She tapped her head. "Imbecile!"

Vali threw back his head, his mirthless laugh echoing against the rock wall. "My plan would have been thwarted had Caol died. De Ros himself declared all hell would break loose if Caol succumbed to his injury. Nay, I did not want the anger of Rose Castle on this Island to deter me from my search. I killed the rebels on the beach to ensure that."

"Yet the fourth man on the beach, you have allowed him to live!" Sheridan pulled the knife from her boot and lunged at him. "Hypocrite!" Twas a moment of satisfaction when the tip of the dagger stabbed his hand as he snatched it from her grip.

Vali hauled her toward the boat, dragging her along as she stumbled to keep pace with him. He shoved her into the skiff and Sheridan crawled onto the stern seat, shaken from the altercation with Vali.

"Fool," Vali growled as he sat on the centre seat. He grasped her booted leg and pulled her second knife from its pocket. Grabbing a piece of rope from the bottom of the boat, he gripped her hands. He tied the rope so tightly that in seconds Sheridan could feel her hands becoming numb. He wrapped the end of the rope around the stern thwart. At least he had not found her third knife secured high on her right thigh. Yet, even that thought brought her no comfort.

Vali took hold of the oars. "When my father lay on his deathbed, there were words spoken, just to me, for I would soon be the next Lord of Vali Island."

A drunken, evil man glared at her through blood-shot eyes. Sheridan turned her face away and watched a kittiwake take flight. It squawked loudly. Oh, how she wished it could fly to Caol and tell him of Vali's treachery.

"My father demanded that I protect you. You were a treasure, he said. I wondered why Sheridan of Vali Island required protection."

Sheridan turned in alarm as Vali lowered an oar into the water. Nay, they could not row away yet. *Come Caol, come.* The oar hit the tip of a rock just below the surface. Twould be a wee bit longer before the boat lifted away from the tide pool.

"When I pushed my father to explain this strange request, he told me also of Angel and the secret of your parentage." Vali held the oars just above the water surface. "Indeed, he passed before he could explain to me where Angel dwelled."

Only last eve had Sheridan learned that her parents had discussed this information with Vali the Younger. Would she be living this nightmare if her parents and Vali the Elder, or even Angel had told her about her lineage?

"I tried to find Angel. I asked assistance from your parents." Vali sneered. "They refused to share this information. 'Angel? Sheridan's lost heritage?' They feigned ignorance. When you hid the ponies, my suspicion grew. Were the beasts secreted away with Angel, the one who walks amongst the ponies at night?

Your parents and you all played a very fine game of hide and seek this summer. Indeed I tried to protect you. Twas only last night when Justus De Ros appeared on the Island that I saw the perfect opportunity to push for the truth."

Vali dipped the oars into the water and the skiff moved smoothly through the waves. A shiver ran along Sheridan's back as a cold chill wrapped around her. Vali's icy stare held no negotiation. He was taking her away from this dear Island, from those she loved. From Caol.

Sheridan leaned forward looking hard at Vali. Perhaps she could penetrate his drunkenness and snatch on to a bit of reasoning. "The ponies have been returned. And you have found Angel."

"As you say, I did find the man in the cave. I had planned to kill him but he shared with me a most peculiar story that he heard on the ships. There is a reward for the capture of you and yours. I spared him for he is of use to me. He has been given charge of the white woman," Vali snarled. He pushed the oars forward, leaning back and straightening his legs. The boat moved away from the tide pool and glided slowly alongside the rock wall.

"The Elder spoke not of the gold. Indeed, I am convinced he knew naught of it. Last eve, I could see that even Ferna and Alan were amazed to see Angel's blanket shimmer with gold. Angel had kept it a secret all these years. The deceiver!" Vali heaved the oars hard and now the boat sped forward quickly.

Too fast now. Sheridan could see the point of the inlet. There, the rock wall dropped down into the open waters. This boat would soon float smoothly away into the bay and the white mist that hovered above it. Caol would never see them.

"After leaving your croft last night, I rowed out to the large ship anchored off the Island. Twas a Norwegian ship. We shared drinks and tales of truth or lies, tis hard to know at times. I told your story. All pretend, I insisted. But nay, an old sailor swore my story is true. There is a fine reward, he said, for anyone who finds the woman and her daughters. Twas the same story the rebel in the cave told." Vali's malicious grin rose higher on his face. "A lie was wrought on the night that your mother and sisters shipwrecked upon this shore. For treasure was to be had if any of you were captured and returned to the place from where you fled. All these years, your Angel has hidden your true story. One of wealth. For there is more to be had from where the gold bits have come. A reward awaits."

"Nay Vali. Angel is not a deceiver. You are. And you know not the way to this place where a reward awaits." Sheridan longed to reach out and touch the rock wall as they sailed by its point. A final farewell to this dear place.

"The rebel and I, we made a pact. We will work together to claim the reward. The white woman will show us the way. For that old sailor claims that the white woman knows from where she has come. She is our guarantee that you will indeed cooperate with us or she will be harmed." Vali sneered. "Twas this Island that cared for you, Sheridan, nurtured you to good health. Called you a daughter. My father cared for Angel and yet she refused to share the knowledge of your background, your wealth."

"Vali, what will you tell the Island folk about my disappearance? You cannot do this, Vali."

"You have played a game of hide and seek all summer. You ran again from us last night, Sheridan. They will see this too as one of your stunts. You have run away, for good."

Sheridan's heart hurt. Looking back at the shore that was slowly left behind, she swallowed down her growing hysteria.

Twas no choice at all.

Chapter Nineteen

Sheridan was gone!

Why was he not surprised? She had given him her word and . . . Caol pushed a hand through his hair and scanned the area. Indeed he was a fool. "A besotted fool!" he muttered. He had believed her and had taken her words to his heart . . . *Never will I leave you.*

An empty basket and the remains of a small fire were the only signs that Sheridan had actually been here. She and Angel had worked through the evening, stitching her clothes, bringing them back to life with embroidered designs. The last he had checked on them, they had fallen asleep beside the low burning fire. He had believed all was well. Even the crimson dotted butterflies had sat contentedly on the hem of Sheridan's skirt again. He had chosen not to disturb them, let them sleep. Surely no one could get by him and harm them.

Caol kicked the charred remains of the fire, causing the ashes to burst upward. He scooped a handful of the ashes, caressing them and then let them fall through his fingers to the ground. The heat had long since vanished.

Caol stood and glared at the old soddie door that hung precariously from its beam. How were Sheridan and Angel able to bypass him? He had sat at the top of the path all night. He and Iain Campbell had taken turns keeping watch. He had checked on Sheridan and Angel approximately an hour past. Both had been asleep.

Caol scanned the area, anger growing in his gut. Sheridan must have run off in this last hour. Deceiver. "Her words are but rot!" he growled. If he could have, he would have kicked himself in the arse. "A fool and fooled."

Instead, he kicked the basket that sat a few feet from the charred remains. It flew high into the air, dumping a few colourful threads to flutter about in the early morning breeze. As the basket twirled a final somersault, a long thread spiralled from it and landed in a clump of weeds. Caol frowned, narrowing his eyes at the colourful threads still floating in the air. Then he slid his gaze to the clump of weeds. Twas no long thread sitting in that clump. Twas the necklace!

A few strides and a swipe of his hand through

the patch of weeds and he held the wooden heart between his fisted fingers. Looking up into the sky, he closed his eyes, thinking carefully. He released his anger.

Caol slid the necklace over his head. Sheridan had not disappeared from this spot willingly. Nay. She had been forced from this spot. Twas no happenstance that the necklace was here but Sheridan was not. Twas a warning, left by her. Something was terribly amiss.

"Campbell!" Caol swung around and faced Iain Campbell who stood beside the far wall of the croft. "Sheridan is missing. And Angel." Scanning the area, he shook his head. "They have been taken." Puzzled, he was, to figure how her assailants had absconded with her.

"Nay! It cannot be," Campbell insisted, scanning the area. "Tis impossible to sneak past us on the trail."

Twas true. Sheridan and whoever had taken her could not have walked the path from this spot. But surely the path was the only way off this plateau. Unless . . . Caol ran toward the old forgotten trail that led down the side of the cliff to the sea. Hot rage gripped him. "Bloody hell! Campbell!"

Two skiffs bobbed in the water below, one was floating past the rock cliff on which Caol stood. The other was slowly gliding directly below him and would soon be clear of the rock wall and its dangers.

Caol turned to Iain Campbell and pointed to the first skiff. "The white woman, Angel. She rides in that boat. She is yours to aid. Do with her assailant as you see fit."

Campbell charged down the path, falling on his knees at one juncture and tumbled along the broken stones. Finally he clambered to his feet and disappeared around a bend in the trail.

Caol rested his hands at his belt, his legs planted wide as he studied the skiff below as it glided out of an inlet toward the bay. He would recognize Sheridan from any distance. She sat in the stern, her hands strangely held in front of her. He was sure her hands were tethered to the stern thwart. A sliver of joy pushed through his rage and wrapped around his heart. She had not left him willingly.

Caol slid his gaze to the man who rowed the boat. "Vali?" Bloody hell! He had taken Sheridan! He watched as Sheridan leaned forward, urgency in her posture, to talk to Vali. He saw Vali grab Sheridan by the front of her cape and push her back. But for her tethered hands, she would have tumbled off her seat.

Fury spurred Caol forward. He stepped down onto the old worn pathway, skidding along the broken stones. He swiped up a piece of cloth along the trail.

Sheridan's headband! He tucked it into a fold of his cape. Then he stepped off the path, ran down an incline and stood at the edge of a lower cliff. He sneered at the cowardly deceiver who rowed the skiff. Vali had become a pox on this Island.

Caol forced down the surge of rage, so poignant and raw, and breathed heavily. For certain, when he got his hands on Vali he would give him tenfold punishment for his treatment of Sheridan. He squeezed his fist tightly, imagining his hands at Vali's neck . . . nay, he had to direct his anger, his energy, to Sheridan's rescue.

Caol determined his descent to the skiff, measuring his plan against the rising waters and the speed of the boat. The tide was already high, and Vali carefully guided the skiff alongside the rock wall of the inlet. The open waters beyond the inlet were deep and clear of jutting rocks. The moment for retribution was drawing nigh. At the moment when the small boat glided beyond the inlet and into the bay, Caol would act.

Caol kept his gaze on the boat as he commanded the calm and focus necessary when preparing for battle. He removed his cape, studying his wife. Sheridan sat so still, shoulders hunched now, head down. *I will fight for you, protect you.* He unbuckled his sword, wrapping its belt about the scabbard and placed it beside his cape. He removed his De Ros plaid, folding it reverently. Twas a finely woven cloth. Indeed, each warrior wore his proudly on his back and was wrapped in his plaid at his burial. Caol placed it on his cape then reverently positioned his scabbard on top of the pile of folded garments.

Caol stood tall, his shoulders back and gazed down into the dark rising water. The boat drew closer to the open waters. The wind fluttered about the hem of Caol's tunic, lifted the ends of his hair and caressed his knees above his boots. It whispered at his ears, mayhap a final benediction for his life.

The warrior raised his arms outward, measuring his launch against the jutting wall of the cliff. As he extended his arms to the sky, he heard the rhythmic boom of the waves, a drum roll calling him into battle. Just as Vali maneuvered the nose of the skiff into the open water, the warrior pushed himself from the cliff. He dove head first toward the dark waters.

Caol sliced through the surface of the turbulent water, sinking deep into its depths. Looking up, satisfaction embraced him. The white skies above silhouetted the hull of the boat well. He had dove into the water in front of the bow of the boat. Vali's was facing the stern and likely had heard the splash but had not seen Caol's entry. But Sheridan, who sat facing the bow, had seen his dive. Hopefully she would feign no knowledge of what caused the splash.

Slowly, Caol edged upward, breaking through the surface of the water and spotted Sheridan. She was looking up at a kittiwake that squawked loudly. When she lowered her gaze and looked out on the water, he rose higher so that his head was fully above the surface. She saw him. There was a slight movement in her posture. When he put a finger to his mouth, she shifted her gaze to another spot.

Caol measured his distance from the boat. With several breast strokes Caol moved toward the bow. Just as the boat came within an arm's length of him, Caol kicked his legs and heaved himself up onto the gunwale. He reached up and grabbed Vali around the neck, dragging him backwards into the water.

Caol pulled the struggling man deep into the wake. Holding him from behind, Caol tightened both arms around Vali's neck. He clasped his hands together at Vali's nape to ensure the man could not break from the hold. Vali's arms and legs flailed about. He pulled at Caol's arms and attempted to snag his legs with Caol's to break the hold.

A streak of pain slashed across Caol's right thigh. A knife! Then Vali was stabbing the knife upward, over his shoulder, toward Caol's face. Twas no satisfaction when Caol added pressure around

Vali's neck and even considered twisting it to the side. Nay, the man would live and pay for his deeds before Scotland's Royal Court. Caol squeezed until the man's body stilled, his limbs floating outward. A single knife glided slowly past his head and then drifted down into the dark depths of the water.

Caol broke through the surface of the water, gasping for air. He dragged the unconscious man to the boat and hoisted him upward so that he hung over the bow. He reached into the boat and swiped a piece of rope lying in the hull. Vali stirred briefly as his hands were tied behind his back.

Caol gripped the gunwale with both hands and rested his forehead against the it. His exhausted body floated in the water, caressed by the waves and the turbulent waters below.

"Caol?"

Sheridan's voice, a rhythmic stroke across his heart, pulled him from his weariness. There was only one thing he wanted to do at this moment.

Caol hoisted himself over the gunwale and swiped a dagger from his boot. He sliced the rope at Sheridan's wrists and gathered her into his arms.

"Thank God you have come." She pushed the wet hair from his face and she snuggled closer to him on the bench where they sat. "He was taking me to a big ship and he talked about a reward for my capture."

Sheridan struggled to sit up and peer beyond the boat into the white mist. "Angel! Tis the man who ran into the cave that took her."

"Shh. Sheridan. All is well." Caol stroked a hand along her back and rested it at her waist, waiting for her heartbeat and his heartbeat, to calm. "Campbell is handling Angel's accomplice."

When she looked up from where she rested her head on his chest, he nodded. "Campbell is very crafty. He will get the job done." He kissed the top of Sheridan's head and caressed her cheek.

Caol's gaze fell on Vali. Water dripped from his mouth and nose. The villain's eyes fluttered open then closed again. He was slowly gaining consciousness. Caol released Sheridan and reached for Vali to haul him fully into the boat. He tied Vali securely at the ankles too. "We must row this boat to the Island," Caol said. "Before it gets too far out to sea."

How he longed to hold Sheridan again and to reassure himself that she lived. Dear God, he had almost lost her forever. He fingered the necklace around his neck and then tugged it off. If he had not found the necklace, he might have believed she had run away from him.

Caol placed the necklace around Sheridan's neck and pulled her closer for just a moment. "Forever the keeper of your heart," he whispered.

Chapter Twenty

Sheridan snuggled into Caol's embrace, leaning back against him. They sat in the shadow of a rock ledge, out of sight from others yet with full view of the happenings. After much singing, dancing and eating, now people quietly mingled about the bonfire. Justus De Ros laughed with Alan and Ferna. Iain Campbell stood alone drinking his ale.

The season had not fully ended, yet the Island Council had decided to celebrate the autumn solstice earlier than usual in celebration of Sheridan's departure from the Island. In this way, all Islanders could bid her a warm farewell. Tomorrow morning, she and Caol would venture to mainland Scotland and on to Rose Castle.

"We will have a similar celebration when we arrive home." Caol placed a flurry of kisses close to Sheridan's ear and a shiver of anticipation for what the night would hold sprung low in her stomach. "I hope you have found enough rest in these past days to be prepared for the greeting you will receive from my people."

To be sure, since Vali's attempt to snatch her and Angel from the Island, Sheridan had found more rest in these few days than in the entire fortnight of her marriage. Mama had insisted that Caol rest quietly in the croft for a few more day. "A measure of peace and quiet will heal what ails you," she had declared as she sutured the slash across his thigh and the wound at his back that had torn open again. They had been left to themselves in their shuttered croft, Sheridan tending to Caol, talking with him, sleeping with him.

Last evening into the wee hours of the night, some Islanders had played instruments and sang outside of their croft. Twas a merry tradition on the Island to try and disturb a newly married couple. Yet the people had altered it and had not demanded entry to the croft. Rather they had sung and played softly in kindness. Most Islanders had been present at the Council hearing for Vali and the people had recognized that she and Caol required rest and healing from the ordeal.

"Do you think Vali's punishment will be of benefit?" Sheridan turned her head to look up at her husband. Warmth spread across her breast as he peered down at her.

"My Scottish tradition would insist that Vali be brought before the Scottish Royal Court and be held accountable before King James himself." He tightened his embrace. "For Vali has failed miserably to lead and this Island and its people belong to the Scottish Royal Court." He lifted Sheridan's hand and kissed it. "Yet twas your Island Council's decision to banish Vali to a remote, uninhabited Island. Tis good that the Island Council is seeking Petter to return. Indeed, he will make a fine new Lord of Vali Island." Caol exhaled loudly, his breath rippling across the top of Sheridan's head. "And let us hope that Vali will find redemption and one day be allowed to return to this Island as a better man. I suspect that Vali not having alcohol available to him might mark the beginning of his healing."

"Let us hope." Yet a shiver ran up Sheridan's back at the thought of Vali's cruel and manipulative ways.

"Vali is far away and he cannot hurt you again." When she did not respond, Caol swept his cape around them, only their heads peeking out from above it. "Let us think about this," he whispered as his hand eased up her calf.

"Caol." Sheridan grabbed his hand, giggling. "Tis not proper here, out in the open. And Ferna prescribed quiet for you."

"We are married, wife. Tis verra proper!" He shook off her hand and skimmed it upward to her knee. "And tis what Ferna called for, quiet." He nibbled at her ear. "We will be verra quiet."

To be sure, their laughter drew heads to turn toward them again and they snuggled deeper into the cape, Caol's hand caressing upward to her thigh.

"Tis the Angel of the Island! Tis her! The Angel!" A young lad ran into the light of the bonfire, waving his arms excitedly. "The Angel of the Island walks with the ponies, for certain!" A few of the merry-makers walked into the night, toward the small pasture where the ponies grazed. Others chuckled and shook their heads at this absurd idea.

"She will have vanished by the time they reach the pasture." Sheridan drew his hand back to her knee. "Dear woman."

"Will Angel ever choose to join in and be part of this Island?" Caol sat up a bit straighter, watching as a few more children disappeared into the darkness toward the pasture. "The land of the living is less lonely."

"Even though I have encouraged her, never will she." Sheridan shrugged. "With her colourless beauty, Angel insists that she is too identifiable to walk amongst the people. As long as I am living, she will remain below the cliff in her rock house. No one saw

Iain Campbell return her to the Island after her rescue. Vali's accomplice is dead and so she is safely hidden again. No one the wiser. " She drew Caol's arms around her, finding comfort and safety within them. "Angel was relieved to hear that even though Vali ranted about the white woman at his Council hearing, no one believed him." Sheridan smiled. "She was quite satisfied that the Council deemed Vali a deranged man."

"In putting the bits and pieces together of your lost heritage, we had thought it was only three sisters hidden twenty years past. But Angel, too, hid. To protect you. Quite a sacrifice." Caol pulled her against his shoulder and whispered. "I promise we will continue to look for your lost heritage. The same promise has been given to Bonnie."

Sheridan snuggled closer to Caol. "Angel is safe. Your foster sister is safe and I am safe." She turned around to face Caol and now straddled him. "It is my hope that someday we might find my third sister and be reassured that she also is safe." She placed Caol's hands on her knees and leaned in to kiss the side of his neck.

"Hmm."

When she looked at Caol, wondering about his sound of disagreement, their noses touched in the dark.

"Sheridan, I would have you completely safe." Caol lifted her off his knee and stood. "Come with me." He pulled her up by the hand.

"Caol? What are you about?" She took quick steps to keep up with Caol's pace as he led her deeper into the shadows and away from the bonfire and villagers. They walked along a path that led to the water hole, turned east and traveled south of Vali the Elder's cairn. The light from the bonfire gleamed far beyond it, setting it aglow. Sheridan smiled. Angel was safe and she was sure the Elder rested in peace now.

Caol led her around the rock plateau and stepped down onto a lower grassy field. Twas where she had hid and watched Vali and Caol days ago. They crossed the field and finally stopped beside the boulder where her rope still hung. She had not been to this place since the day Caol had been wounded on the beach.

Sheridan watched as Caol snatched up the rope and began to pull it hand over hand from the cliff wall. He did not coil the rope as he dragged it up over the edge but let it fall in a heap at his feet. When the end of the rope appeared, Caol pulled a dagger from his boot.

"Sheridan, I would like us to cut this rope, destroy it. Then I know that you will be safe never to climb high cliffs again." Caol held out the end of the rope. "What say you?"

Sheridan took the rope in her hands, caressing it gently, lovingly. Her rope. How could she destroy this dearly woven piece of cord that had brought her many joys throughout her years? Papa had taught her to scale low walls using this rope. She had woven length into this rope with Angel's guidance. She smiled when she thought of the ponies and using this rope to lead them. Nay, she would carry it with her to her new home, Rose Castle.

Sheridan lifted her eyes to Caol. The earnestness of Caol's request had settled in his frown, in the grim set about his mouth. When she shook her head, his brows furrowed above narrowed eyes. "This rope holds wonderful memories, Caol." She hugged the rope to her breast. "Nay, I cannot destroy it."

"Hmm." Caol strode to the cliff edge and looked out into the darkness of the night. He threw his arms wide then dropped them to his sides. "Sheridan you have promised me never to climb cliffs again. This will be the way of holding you to that promise, of guaranteeing your safety, once and for all."

Twas the disappointment coiled about his words and in the way he held his back to her that challenged her to find just the right words to explain her reasoning. Twas too easy to be daunted by her husband's intimidating demand and his threatening stance.

Caol turned to her, placed his hands at his belt and stood with his legs wide. "You must explain to this husband why you cannot destroy that godforsaken rope."

Sheridan began to coil the rope. "Caol," she whispered. "Tis a precious rope, this piece of cord." She kept a steady rhythm of wrapping it around her hand and elbow as she spoke. "For it brought me to you. To be sure, it landed me right into your arms." When she finished coiling the rope, she pulled a knife from her boot and severed the cord from the boulder. "That day, if I had chosen to take the rock stairs to Angel never would we have married." She made a loop in the end of the rope."Twas a splendid day."

"Sheridan . . ."

Just as Caol took a step toward her, Sheridan flung the rope high. It flared above Caol's head and fell down around his body. She cinched it as it snared him around his middle. When he would have spoken, she cinched it a bit tighter and pulled a surprised Caol toward her. She had to smile for it was rare to see her husband speechless. "This is my pledge. This wife's promise to her husband." A final tug and he stood before her. "I will stand with you and fight for us until our days are no more." She lifted the cord from around him and twisted the loose end into the coiled rope.

"Twill be my tradition, my ritual, to be forever the keeper of your heart, Caol." Sheridan rose to her tiptoes and kissed him so tenderly that her eyes pooled with tears. Then she handed him the rope. "And you can be the keeper of our rope."

Caol's eyes twinkled and he chuckled low as he accepted the rope. "My wife is splendid and also sensible." He pushed an arm through the coiled rope and slid it up to his shoulder then he pulled Sheridan close. His mouth lingered for a moment above her lips, caressing them gently.

Oh, how she loved this man. Her heartbeat quickened and a warm flush rose up from her breast. When she snaked her arms around his shoulders, Caol lifted her off the ground and she wrapped her legs about his waist. The night breeze danced around them as slowly Caol caressed beneath her skirt, lifting it higher as he ran his hands along the back of her thighs.

"Tis a chilly night," Sheridan whispered against his neck. "Should we hurry to the croft and build a fire."

Caol lowered her to the ground. "Nay wife. Let us make our own fire right here."

"Expeditiously, husband," she urged, shivering as the cool wind whipped about them.

"Leisurely," Caol whispered against her ear.

When he threw his cape over them, there was such joy in his chuckle and in her giggle.

"Splendid," she breathed.

Epilogue

Lady Brianna squinted, resting a hand above her eyes to shield her view from the late morning sun. She drew her shawl closer to ward off the chill of the cool September morning. She was certain she had seen the tip of a boat's mast bob above the horizon line of the cliff. The blinding rays of the sun disappeared when she stepped into the shadows of a few gnarled trees. For certain, one of the small ships had anchored.

Brianna ran to the top of the path that led down to the large dock where Rose Castle moored its two sea vessels. Her husband, Justus De Ros, had already debarked the boat and was climbing up the path. His dark gaze met hers and Brianna's excitement leapt low in her stomach. She grasped onto her necklace and caressed the wooden heart that dangled from it. From the distance, he appeared well. For certain, all in one piece.

She had been so scared when he left to search for Caol on Vali Island. She had begged him not to go. Their son, Caol, was a capable man, she had argued. Caol could manage on his own. But when her husband had opened his hand and shown her the small wooden heart that Caol had sent to Rose Castle, she knew. De Ros sailed the next day.

When her husband stepped off the path, Brianna wrapped her arms around her him. "Thank goodness. You have arrived back safely," she breathed.

"All is well," he reassured her, placing his forehead against hers to gaze into her eyes.

"For certain?"

"Aye, all is well, my Breeze." And then he smiled.

Away skittered her fear and anxiety. She was always amazed how a smile from De Ros could calm her fears. She had, long ago, stopped wondering how he did that. Brianna took his hands and held them to her breast. "De Ros, I have the best news. For certain, you will never imagine what it—"

A shadow wavered behind De Ros, then someone stepped into her view. "Caol!" Brianna extended her hands and her son stepped closer. "I am so glad to see you. And all in one piece." She rose on her tip-toes and kissed his cheek. "So glad," she repeated.

"Mother." Caol smiled. A twinkle of humour sat in his eyes and then he pulled someone from behind him. A woman stepped out and stood beside him. "Mother, I am happy to introduce you to Sheridan of Vali Island." His smile grew bigger. "My wife."

Brianna's hand flew to her breast. "Your w . . . wife?" she stuttered, looking from her husband to her son. She quickly found her good manners and stepped closer to the young woman. "I have heard many tales of Vali Island, about you and its people over these years." She took the young woman's hand. "Caol's wife?" She shook her head and then gently laughed. "Welcome to our family."

Sheridan's smile did not quite touch her eyes. For certain, she looked quite pale and . . . Brianna took a step closer, gazing at the woman. Strange that she had never met the lass, yet there appeared something familiar about her.

"I thank you for your welcome, Lady Brianna." Sheridan wiped a shaking hand across her brow.

"Mother. We have all learned something new about Sheridan, this day. Although she has floated on rowboats about the Island since her early days, she has never sailed on a large ship." Caol looked at his wife with sympathy and patted her hand. "She was sea sick on the voyage."

"Sea sick?" Brianna knew she should take

Sheridan to the castle and settle her in her new home, yet her feet were somehow stuck to the ground. She could not quite figure it out but she felt she had met this woman, Sheridan of Vali Island, somewhere. For certain, twas impossible!

"Caol, you will . . . you will . . . take Sheridan . . ."

"Not to worry, Mother. I will take Sheridan to the castle and get her settled," Caol reassured, that secretive twinkle still in his eye. "A wee nap and then good food will be the remedy for my sea sick wife." Caol walked away, his arm about Sheridan's waist.

"Breeze?"

"Hmm," Brianna muttered and sat down on an old log. "She seems familiar, she does. But I cannot quite put my finger on why I would think that." She stared after the young couple who had reached the top of the hill, ready to disappear over the knoll.

"Breeze?"

Brianna slid her gaze to De Ros. He held the same secretive twinkle in his eye that Caol had held.

"You look like you have just seen a ghost, Breeze."

Something was amiss. Yet, in this moment, grief and joy danced together in her heart. "I could hardly bear to see our Bonnie leave us this spring." She rubbed her breast. "I thought for a time, the grief might just kill me."

"Breeze," De Ros soothed. He sat down beside her and pulled her closer.

"I know Bonnie is well. That our dear daughter thrives in her new home." Brianna wiped at her wet eyes. "And yet, she was taken from me before I was ready to give her to another." Joy leapt high in her heart and nudged away the grief. "But here on this day, I have been given another daughter." She shook her head in amazement. "Tis a blessing, for certain!"

"Sheridan is a lovely girl. Verra skilled with ponies," De Ros explained. "She will step into Bonnie's place well and will be of great help to—"

Brianna jumped up, arms akimbo, staring at the now deserted hill top. "De Ros!" She turned to him, again meeting that secretive twinkle. She narrowed her eyes at her husband. "De Ros," she challenged. "I would wager that Sheridan is the sister of our Bonnie."

Now De Ros stood, feigning a surprised air. "Nay. It cannot be. Our Bonnie is tall. Sheridan is petite."

"De Ros, that secret behind your eyes is about to pop out!" Brianna could not help but give a quick pinch to his belly.

De Ros chuckled and grabbed her hand, tugging her close. "What say you, Breeze? How have you come to this concocted notion?" He grabbed her other hand when she attempted to pinch him again and brought it to his smiling lips.

"I can hardly believe my eyes. For certain, tis a daughter for a daughter, De Ros." Tears pooled. "A daughter for a daughter. I can hardly believe it."

"How did you know, Breeze? Dear God, I have visited Vali Island every summer for years and never once recognized Sheridan's similarities to Bonnie." He kissed her gently on the lips. "Was it the freckles? Both women have golden sparks in their eyes."

"Tis true. Both share freckles and golden sparks." Brianna stepped away and looked again down the path. "Twas the nose. They both have the same tip to their nose."

"Nose tip?" De Ros laughed.

Brianna twirled around and tapped him on the nose. "Aye, nose tip. Tis as clear as day."

De Ros pulled her into his arms. "Caol and I, we had wondered how long it would take you to figure it out." He chuckled. "We are certain Sheridan is the second of the three sisters. Tis the oldest one that is still lost. But, tis Sheridan's story and she will likely share her tale with you this eve."

De Ros took her hand and turned toward the path that led to the castle. "We got waylaid, aye? And so, what is your good news, Breeze? You were all but bursting with it when you met me at the top of the dock trail?"

Brianna walked beside her husband. She caressed the wooden heart of her necklace. "I think you will have to make another wooden heart. Aye?"

"Nay, Breeze. Tis not my job to make a wooden heart for Sheridan." He tugged his hat lower on his brow, shielding his eyes from the bright sun.

"Hmm," Brianna murmured, smiling up at De Ros. She laughed loudly when he stopped abruptly, his mouth dropping open, his eyes narrowing.

"Breeze?"

"We will need the heart by early spring." She feigned a serious expression, quite pleased to see the twinkle fade from her husband's eye to that of surprise.

"A . . . a bairn, Breeze?" Now it was De Ros' turn to stutter.

"Aye, De Ros." Brianna stepped closer to him, smiling. "Tis my good news." She rose to her tip-toes and wrapped her arms around De Ros' shoulders. "Can you believe it? For certain, we'll have another babe by spring time."

"Tis good news, my Breeze." He drew her closer, resting his forehead against hers, smiling into her eyes. "Another heart to keep, to love."

Brianna kissed her husband's lips and then snuggled into his embrace. For certain, the year had been full of challenges. And blessings. A give and take in many ways. A daughter taken but another given. A son detained on Vali Island but returned safely with a wife. And now a babe grew in her womb. For certain, another heart to love.

She and De Ros turned again to the castle, holding hands as they walked along. Brianna caressed the wooden heart at her neck. Her spirit soared with joy.

Memory Keeper

Coming soon

Book 3 in the **Keeper Trilogy**

Journey with Cayda and Iain Campbell as they fall in love and together solve the mystery of the third sister.

About the Author

Melanie Joye (Climenhage-Nopper) is an educator and writer with experience in elementary and post-Secondary education and holds a Master of Education in Literacy. She lives in Barrie, Ontario, Canada with her family. Melanie enjoys reading biography, history, romance and adventure—themes that are woven into the fabric of her stories. She loves to incorporate into her writings the natural environments where she has lived and which she has explored. In this series, the Keeper Trilogy, the setting is reflective of the Highlands of Haliburton, Ontario and Scotland. As you immerse yourself in these pages, you too will experience the adventure, soak up the rugged beauty and taste the dew of these ancient rocky lands.